The Lighthouse between the Worlds

Also by Melanie Crowder

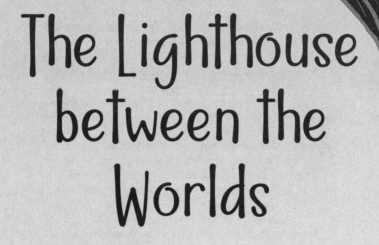

The Lighthouse between the Worlds

Melanie Crowder

Atheneum

Atheneum Books for Young Readers

New York London Toronto Sydney New Delhi

ATHENEUM BOOKS FOR YOUNG READERS
An imprint of Simon & Schuster Children's Publishing Division
1230 Avenue of the Americas, New York, New York 10020
ATHENEUM BOOKS FOR YOUNG READERS is a registered trademark of Simon & Schuster, Inc. Atheneum logo is a trademark of Simon & Schuster, Inc.
For information about special discounts for bulk purchases, please contact Simon & Schuster Special Sales at 1-866-506-1949 or business@simonandschuster.com.
The Simon & Schuster Speakers Bureau can bring authors to your live event. For more information or to book an event, contact the Simon & Schuster Speakers Bureau at 1-866-248-3049 or visit our website at www.simonspeakers.com.
Book design by Debra Sfetsios-Conover
The text for this book was set in Palatino LT.
The illustrations for this book were rendered digitally.
Manufactured in the United States of America
0918 FFG   First Edition   10 9 8 7 6 5 4 3 2 1
Library of Congress Cataloging-in-Publication Data
Names: Crowder, Melanie, author.
Title: The lighthouse between the worlds / Melanie Crowder.
Description: First edition. | New York : Atheneum Books for Young Readers, [2018] | Summary: After discovering that the lighthouse his family tends is a portal to strange and dangerous worlds, eleven-year-old Griffin must travel through it to save his father from a threat to all humanity.
Identifiers: LCCN 2018009077 | ISBN 9781534405141 (hardback) | ISBN 9781534405165 (eBook)
Subjects: | CYAC: Rescues—Fiction. | Magic—Fiction. | Fantasy. | Science fiction. | BISAC: JUVENILE FICTION / Action & Adventure / General. | JUVENILE FICTION / Fantasy & Magic. | JUVENILE FICTION / Science Fiction.
Classification: LCC PZ7.C885382 Li 2018 | DDC [Fic]—dc23
LC record available at https://lccn.loc.gov/2018009077

For the Crowders
Tom and Cara Lee, Lisa and Christina

PART ONE

THE APPRENTICE GLASSMAKER

THE DAY BEGAN NORMALLY enough, for a Tuesday. Griffin and his father, Philip Fenn, ate breakfast (juice and apple-butter toast for one, coffee and oatmeal for the other). They buttoned up their thickest flannel shirts and stepped out into the gray morning. Mornings are almost always gray on the Oregon coast. But that's what makes the green of the mosses and the ferns and the scraggly trees so *very* green.

Father and son tromped up the wooded path leading along the bluff toward the lighthouse. Griffin darted ahead, sucking in his breath and lining his skinny shoulders up with the rough bark of an obliging tree trunk. The seconds ticked by as he waited for his dad to catch up, anticipation bubbling up and threatening to spill over. Griffin leaped out just as his father lunged toward his hiding spot—they both howled in surprise—and the chase began, darting and winding through the rain-spattered woods. When they broke through the trees, gasping for breath between fits of laughter, the stark red roof and tall white tower of the lighthouse stood out from the green-gray ocean and the blue-gray sky as if to say *Look at me. Pay attention.*

It was the Fenn family's job to care for the aging building. Philip was a glassmaker who looked after the delicate prisms in the lens that swiveled high in the tower day in and day out, sending powerful beams of light sweeping over the mighty Pacific. The grassy landing also boasted two sheds that had once been used to store oil for powering the light above. These days, one held rakes, shovels, and a temperamental lawnmower, while the other had been remade into the family glassmaking studio.

Instead of a more traditional fifth-grade classroom, school for Griffin was here, right beside his dad. This morning's lesson was on casting prisms. Philip wrote the equation for the ratio of silica, soda, and lime on the chalkboard, and Griffin moved through the steps, measuring out the ingredients, then melting, raking, and cooling the molten glass. The following day, he'd grind, measure, and grind again until he'd gotten the angles just right. The two worked together, and father peppered son with questions all the while.

When the lesson was finished, they went for a walk on the beach. Philip skipped stones on the fan of waves receding with the outgoing tide while Griffin combed through the flotsam strewn across the sand, hunting for a piece of sea glass. Then they hiked up the bluff to his mother's grave, the somber note that was always there, beneath the rest, rising to the surface.

Griffin clasped his father's hand as they drew near. There was no headstone, only a suncatcher Griffin had made to soften the sunlight's fall on that particular rectangle of earth. And then, like he did every day, he set the tumbled shard of glass he'd found on the beach below into the ever-expanding frame.

After lunch (SpaghettiOs for one and a tuna sandwich for the other), Griffin and his father oiled the ancient brass gears that rotated the lens high in the lighthouse tower. It was a first order Fresnel lens with eight panels of thick greenish glass that tapered up toward the domed ceiling of the lantern room and down to the grated steel floor. Around the middle, eight panels of concentric circles like bull's-eyes channeled the light from a single bulb into beams that shone twenty-one miles out to sea. It was magnificent! And right at that moment, the lens didn't even need the clouds to part and let the sun through; all that glass sparkled and winked on its own.

Griffin and his father stepped out onto the gallery and squeegeed the windows. The wind flicked at the soapy bubbles and dribbled the wash water down their forearms. Philip carefully drew his wand down the glass, while Griffin swooped and squiggled over his dad's straight, measured lines.

When they'd finished, father and son closed up the lighthouse for the day and tripped back down the path to the old keeper's cottage, where they warmed their toes by the sitting room fire, sipping piping hot mugs of cocoa (with bobbing mini marshmallows in one and a nip of whiskey in the other).

Griffin licked a melted-marshmallow mustache off his upper lip and watched some nasty weather roll in off the water. The dingy furniture in the sitting room was angled so you could be warmed by the fire and take in the view at the same time. The walls were covered in nautical wallpaper dotted with a few dusty oil paintings, a barometer, an antique clock, and a shelf of books that listed slightly to the left. A dozen guidebooks were stacked on the shelf, containing more information than you'd need in several lifetimes on things like mariner's knots, tide pools, whale migration patterns, and seabird watching. On the shelf below the books perched an ancient weather radio that frequently emitted a low hum of chatter announcing Coast Guard dispatches and storm alerts. Beneath the radio was a small locked cupboard.

Griffin and his father hardly had any visitors, and they went out of their way to avoid the tourists who veered off the highway to get a closer look at the lighthouse. A just-the-two-of-them kind of quiet filled their days. It may have been a strange sort of life for a kid, but it suited Griffin just fine.

After all, he was doing important work; he was an apprentice in the family trade. It was glass that had brought his parents together—she a PhD student in anthropology, specializing in the impact of the material's first contact with societies around the globe, and he a skilled tradesman working in restoration. The couple had moved to the coast so Katherine could study the effect of the Fresnel lens on maritime culture up and down the country's western coast and so Philip could be on hand to tend the lighthouse and repair the glass panels if need be.

At least, that's what Griffin had always been told. It never occurred to him to wonder if there was more to the story.

2

A LOCK AND A KEY

THERE ARE SOME noises that will make a person jump right out of his skin. A foghorn on an ocean liner, for example. The whistle on a train. Or a tsunami siren when it winds up to its hair-raising wail.

Just when the warmth of the cocoa and the fire had Griffin practically melting into the sofa cushions, an ear-splitting alarm screeched through the sitting room. The mug flew out of his hands, and if there had been any cocoa left inside, it would have soaked the faded rug at his feet.

Philip jumped up. (His cocoa *did* splash across the rug, and halfway up the wall, too.) He hurdled over the back of the sofa and knelt beside the locked cupboard. He unclipped the multi-purpose knife at his waist and pried off the handle's plastic cover.

Beneath, a small key lay within a foam bed molded exactly to its shape. Philip inserted the key into the lock, twisted it, and yanked the cupboard door open. Inside was a brown box encased in leather, with a single silver toggle at its center. He flipped the toggle down and back up again, and the alarm stopped as abruptly as it had begun.

While his father leaped into action, shock rooted Griffin to that very spot. He stared openmouthed at the cupboard, his hands clamped over his ears. He walked past it several times a day, hardly even noticing the locked door or considering what might lie behind it.

Philip drew a hand across the salt-and-pepper stubble on his jaw. There was a decision to be made. He was left with only two options, and both were terrible.

The fire crackled pleasantly as if nothing out of the ordinary had happened. Drips of spilled cocoa slid down the wallpaper. Outside, above the restless winter ocean, heavy clouds crept toward the shore.

"Dad?" There was hardly enough moisture in Griffin's mouth for that one syllable. He swallowed and tried again. "What was that?"

Philip's voice was muffled, his fist jammed against his lips. He didn't turn to meet his son's eyes. "It's a warning."

"What do you mean? What kind of warning?" Unease snapped and popped through Griffin like a flame sputtering along a fuse.

Philip leaned over, reached into the cupboard a second time, and pulled out a thin journal. The corners were dented inward, and the linen cover was faded with age. He tucked it into the back pocket of his jeans and tugged the curved edge of his flannel shirt down to hide it. Philip dropped a reassuring arm over his son's shoulders, but he flinched a little when he finally met Griffin's worried gaze.

"We don't have time for me to tell you everything—there's too much—and anyway, they'll be here any minute."

"*Who* will be here?"

"The Keepers."

"Who?"

But Philip only strode to the front door and peered outside, waiting. It wasn't that he didn't know the answers to Griffin's questions, or that he was avoiding them. A singular dread had fallen over him, and it rang in his ears louder than that hateful alarm. The truth was that Philip would have taken the tsunami siren any day. *That* he could do something about—he could heft his son onto his back and sprint to higher ground.

But this? He couldn't run from this.

Philip had done everything he could to warn the Keepers that this might happen. But they hadn't done a single thing he'd suggested. They'd barely listened to him. Philip closed his eyes and leaned his forehead against the cottage door. Maybe none of it mattered. He knew all too well that no matter how thoroughly you prepare or how desperately you try, sometimes you can't protect the ones you love most.

VISITORS

IN ADDITION TO the occasional spouting gray whale, passing trawler, or frolicking sea lion, the picture windows of the Fenn cottage were witness to a host of air travelers. Hordes of gulls, the occasional eagle, and at least once a day, one of those big orange Coast Guard helicopters zoomed by. But Griffin had never imagined one would drop from the sky and land on the cottage lawn.

He ran to the window and craned his neck for a better look. The orange belly lowered closer and closer to the ground, and for the second time that afternoon Griffin clamped his hands over his ears to muffle the sound. On any other day, he would have dashed outside, jumping up and down, waving at the crew and hollering for his dad to join him. But on this

day, after that piercing alarm and the too-quiet minutes that had followed, anything out of the ordinary
seemed sure to be horrible. Griffin hurried over to his
father's side.

A spray of sand blasted the cottage windows,
and the helicopter swayed in a sudden gust of wind
before the landing gear touched down. The rotors
slowed, and out poured a dozen grown-ups wearing
identical pale blue pajama-like outfits. They leaned
into the wind, the red sashes cinched around their
waists fluttering like kite tails behind them, and they
marched toward the cottage.

Philip opened the door with a grimace, stepping
in front of Griffin and shielding the boy as the strangers tromped inside. There were eight of them, following behind a woman whose silver hair swept over
her shoulder in a long, loose braid.

"Well, Philip," she said in a brisk tone. "It would
seem that you were right."

They didn't have many visitors at the cottage—
just Griffin's grandparents, who came on his birthday every year. He peered around his father's arm,
curiosity getting the better of him. The woman standing toe-to-toe with his dad held her hand out to the
side, and a folded set of the same funny blue clothes
was placed into her upturned palm.

"You'd better get dressed," she said in the kind of tone that suggested she was used to giving orders and used to having them obeyed.

Philip crossed his arms over his button-down flannel. He wasn't a tall man, but after years of work in the glass studio, his frame was sturdy and strong. "No, Hypatia. I'll show you what to do, but this time you're on your own."

The woman puffed her cheeks in exasperation. "You're our best candidate—"

"Absolutely not. My family has sacrificed enough."

Sacrificed? Griffin searched his dad's face for answers. What were they talking about? And why did he look so scared?

"Come now," the woman said. "We all wish Katherine had—"

"Stop it!" Philip shouted, his whole body trembling. "You don't get to say her name to me."

Griffin wrapped both arms around his dad's waist and held tight. He didn't understand what was going on, but his dad's grief, still raw after three long years—that was as familiar as his own skin. That's the way it is when you've lost someone. The grief is always right there, below the surface.

"But they are tampering with the lens." Hypatia enunciated as if she were speaking to a small child.

"The portal might open at any moment. We *need* you."

"No, you needed to listen when I warned you year after year that this would happen. But you didn't, did you? So, no. I'm not going anywhere. My son needs me."

At that moment all eyes shifted to Griffin. He stepped forward, crossing his arms over his chest, an echo of his father's defiant stance. "Go away. We don't want you here."

Griffin and his father were different people. When they played checkers, Griffin hopped his pieces all over the board, while Philip marched his forward in strategic chevrons. Griffin squished all the foods together on his dinner plate—the gravy and the peas drowning in heaps of mashed potato, while the dividing lines on Philip's plate were never, *ever* breached. The two of them weren't the same. But when what remained of the Fenn family was confronted with a threat from the outside, they faced it together.

And from what Griffin had seen so far? These people were a threat.

Hypatia leaned closer to get a better look at Griffin. He had round brown eyes set into pale skin and thick brown hair that twisted and curled at the edges, barely leaving room for details like eyebrows and earlobes to peek through. Whether it was from the chill outside, or the unusual events of the afternoon, the tops of his cheeks flushed bright red.

The woman pursed her lips as if she had swallowed something sour. "I'm guessing you don't remember me. I'm Dr. Hypatia Hibbert."

Griffin stared straight back. Dr. Hibbert's face was all angles—hard eyebrows and sharp cheekbones. And a long, thin nose. Even if this had been an ordinary day, with no blaring alarms or helicopters dropping out of the sky, even if he hadn't heard the way his dad's voice broke when Dr. Hibbert spoke his mother's name, *that* wasn't the kind of face that made a person feel at ease.

She extended her hand to shake, but Philip was having none of it. He stepped into the entryway, pulling Griffin with him. "You know the way." He threw the door open, ignoring the wind that gusted in and the rain that splattered over everything.

Dr. Hibbert sniffed. She lifted her chin and sailed outside. The rest of the grown-ups followed her down the porch steps and up the forested path to the lighthouse. Philip hugged his son tight and watched them go. And that would have been that if the alarm hadn't suddenly started blaring again for the second time that day. Griffin jumped. His father ground his teeth together.

"Dad!" Griffin shouted over the racket. "What is going on?" Unease prickled along his skin, and his palms began to sweat. There was supposed to be an order to their days, a pattern of work and rest and play. It was predictable. Safe. Comforting. And Griffin liked it that way.

Philip stood in the open doorway. The wind whipped the tails of his flannel and tugged at the ends of his hair. His face broke and he knelt, taking his son by the shoulders.

Griffin knew his father better than anyone else in the world. He could always feel one of those big belly laughs coming on before Philip's shoulders even began to shake. He knew the kind of stillness that would come over him when he was remembering the time before the accident, before Katherine had died. But the look in his dad's eyes right then was something Griffin had never seen before.

"I have to go."

The alarm shrieked from inside the cupboard.

"What do you mean?" Griffin's voice was barely above a squeak. "Where are you going?"

"I just need to make a quick adjustment to the lens. I've been working on a block for this side of the por—" Philip cut himself off, shaking his head in frustration. "There isn't time to explain. Griffin,

I hoped this would never happen. But I have to go help them."

"Then I'm coming with you."

"No. It's too dangerous. You need to stay here. I'll be right back."

"Dangerous?" Griffin's voice wavered. His dad wasn't supposed to go running off without him. "I don't understand."

"I'm sure it seems like you don't. But the truth is, you know more than you think you do. Everything I've told you about the lighthouse, and working glass—it's all part of this mess. When I get back, I'll fill in the gaps. I'll tell you everything I know."

Griffin didn't like it. He scraped his thumbnail against the calluses that scarred his palm, the hard layer straining against the soft one surrounding it. "Keep the walkie-talkie with you."

"I should only be up at the lighthouse for a few minutes. Unless . . ." Philip winced. He reached into his back pocket and pulled out the journal. He thumbed to the back and pried out a sprig of green from beneath a clear plastic flap. He unbuttoned his sleeve and thrust it up over his elbow. Philip carefully laid the vine's tip against his pale forearm. The plant seemed to soften as it touched his skin, and he lowered the rest of the vine, bit by bit, along the narrow blue vein that ran up his arm.

The plant faded, dissolving into his skin. "What *is* that?" Griffin reached out and grabbed Philip's arm, but the vine was gone, his skin smooth and unmarked. *"Dad."*

Griffin blinked. Sure, plants moved in the wind or when rain splattered against their leaves, and if you had nothing to do all day besides sit in one spot and watch them follow the sun across the sky or inch upward, you'd see a little shift. But that vine had slid like a garden snake over his dad's arm.

Philip shook out his sleeve and buttoned it closed once more. He knelt down, holding the journal out to Griffin. "Will you hang on to this for me? Don't show it to anyone, no matter what they say."

Griffin's fingers curled around the thin book. Questions crowded into his mind, each new one shoving the last out of the way to make room. The uneasy feeling he hadn't been able to shake since that helicopter touched down turned over into something that felt a lot more like dread. "Dad? I'm scared."

Philip drew Griffin close. The alarm blared. Rain pummeled Philip's shoulders and splattered against Griffin's face. Philip pulled back, took a long look at his son, and then wrenched himself away.

Griffin stepped into the open doorway, leaning

into the wind and watching as his father disappeared up the path leading to the lighthouse. He didn't notice the rain soaking through his flannel and weighing the thick fabric down until goose bumps rose on his skin and his whole body began to shake.

"It's just the cold," he said to the air, as if speaking the words aloud would make them true. He shut the door on the wind and the rain and the knowledge that he didn't believe that, not for a second.

SOLID GLASS

GRIFFIN FLICKED THE toggle on the strange box in the cupboard, stopping the alarm mid-screech. The house went quiet. Too quiet after everything that had happened, as if it, too, was stunned into silence. Griffin glanced anxiously around the empty sitting room. His dad was going to be right back. Any minute. Wasn't he?

It wasn't like Philip to leave his son behind. That wasn't how the Fenn family did things. Griffin pulled a crocheted blanket over his shoulders and crossed to the window, peering north to where the lighthouse stood, braced for impact, on a bluff overlooking ocean waves that crashed into the rocks below. On winter days like this one, jealous storms flooded the beach to the south, ripping up the sand, churning it far away from shore, and leaving shredded jellyfish and long ropes of kelp in its place.

Griffin turned the journal over in his hands. It was too big to fit in the pockets of his jeans. He drew in a shallow breath. The way those strangers had stormed into the cottage like they owned the place, he didn't think it would stay hidden under his pillow or even in the secret pocket in the lining of his backpack. He needed to keep it on him, somewhere no one could see it, at least until his dad got back. Then they could make a better plan, together.

He drifted upstairs and dug through the first aid kit in the hall closet. A mountain of Ace bandages toppled off the shelf and rolled down the hallway, bumping down the stairs with muted thuds. He found what he was looking for way at the back, under an electric heating pad. It was a pouch with an elastic strap that his dad used to ice his back sometimes. Griffin slid the journal into the pouch and cinched it around his waist, lowering his flannel shirt over the top. He ducked into his bedroom and stood in front of the full-length mirror, twisting to the right and then the left. He nodded, satisfied. You couldn't tell anything was under there.

Griffin checked the clock above his mirror. He bit his lip. He should have made his dad take him along.

Griffin glanced at the clock a second time. They'd only been gone a few minutes. But what if his dad needed Griffin's help?

And who were those people anyway? Griffin's eyes caught on the reflection in the mirror of his messy bedroom—his rumpled sheets, the uneven stack of library books, and the wall opposite where he stood. Griffin turned slowly, the hairs on the back of his neck rising until they stood on end. The wall was covered with papers—a patchwork of his mother's drawings. There were all sorts: atmospheric pastels, detailed pen-and-ink drawings, silly sketches, and sweeping imagined landscapes that didn't look like anything you'd find on Earth.

Sometimes Griffin's mom had told him bedtime stories to go with the drawings, like the one with the singing ocean, or the one about the world with a city in the sky. Griffin didn't care if it was all nonsense he should have grown out of years ago. They were hers. Each drawing had lived in his mother's mind and found its way onto paper through her fingers.

Griffin crept closer. In the center of the wall hung a portrait his eyes must have glossed over a hundred times. It was a moody charcoal sketch of a middle-aged woman with a loose braid snaking over her shoulder. The eyes seemed to glitter, and the lips were drawn into a thin, disapproving line.

He knew that face.

Griffin stumbled backward as the realization seared into him, like when you step on a half-buried sea urchin. The spines stab through your skin and set their barbs—you don't even see it until the pain starts ripping through you.

A long-forgotten memory rose up, playing over his vision as if it were happening right there, in front of his eyes. That same alarm had sounded once before, three years ago. Griffin's mother and father had rushed to shut it off, their bodies stiff with panic and their eyes wide with fear. Though Katherine had just returned from a work trip the day before (and she usually stayed put for a few months after anything that took her away from her family), she'd left again in a hurry that very evening. A week later, Griffin and his father had stood hand in hand at her funeral.

Griffin sputtered, his lungs forcing a breath before the rest of him was ready to be jolted back to the present. The last time that awful alarm had sounded, Griffin had lost his mother. And now the woman in the sketch—Dr. Hibbert—showed up, and his dad rushed off in a panic, just like his mom had done all those years ago.

Griffin tore out of his room. He was not going to lose his dad, too. He leaped downstairs and grabbed the walkie-talkie off the sideboard. "Dad, can you hear me? Pick up!" He checked the channel. He banged the battery pack against his palm and adjusted the volume. "Dad?" But no answer came from the lighthouse, only static. Griffin slammed the walkie-talkie back onto the charger.

It was one thing to be nervous around those strangers. But now he was scared. Griffin yanked his raincoat off its hook and pulled it over his shoulders as he bounded down the front-porch steps.

Griffin sprinted up the path that wove through a stand of wind-beaten Sitka spruce. In the gaps between trees, the ocean roared. Branches slapped at his knees as he raced by, the fading light glinting off damp leaves and waterlogged soil. A bird with slick black feathers shot out of the bushes lining the path, flapping its wings and twisting frantically to get out of Griffin's way.

When he reached the lighthouse, Griffin pushed through the workroom door and darted up the spiral stairs. He panted for breath, hauling himself up the steps two at a time. A hum vibrated through the curved brick walls and rattled his teeth. Around and around and up and up he ran. The crowd of strangers

huddled together on the watch room landing, staring at the lens rotating in the lantern room above. Griffin shoved past them, reaching for the railing.

Dr. Hibbert peered down at the boy as he passed. "Sykes—" She barely bothered to raise her voice.

Griffin was halfway up the stairs when someone grabbed him from behind and yanked him back down. "Dad!" Griffin struggled to break free, but the hands only gripped tighter.

"Let me go!" Griffin kicked Sykes in the shins, and when that didn't do any good, he tried the knees.

The floor above them was made up of thick steel with clusters of holes in each segment, letting light down into the watch room and giving anyone standing below a dappled view of the lantern room. Griffin could just make out his father kneeling in front of the center panel in the lens and struggling to remove the line of rivets holding the glass in place.

All day, every day, the floor-to-ceiling lens rotated, sending its powerful beams out to sea. Except, at that moment nothing moved, not the gears in the watch room, not the lens above, and not Griffin's dad. Everything was eerily still. And then the bull's-eye right in front of Philip shifted. What should have been a thick pane of solid glass began to swirl like liquid.

"Dad!" Griffin screamed. He struggled to wrest free of Sykes's grip.

Philip jerked at the sound of his son's voice. He pulled back, turning away from the lens, his eyes searching the floor below for Griffin. He was almost to the stairs when the bull's-eye seemed to reach out for him, the green glass circles stretching like salt-water taffy until they thrust through Philip's chest in a ring of light.

Philip's eyes bulged wide. His movements slowed even as he strained toward his son. The tips of his hair and edges of his clothes thinned until they were translucent, and the humming intensified to a rattle.

"Griffin!" he cried. "Griffin, I'm so sorry!"

And suddenly the liquid glass snapped back, yanking Philip with it, his arms and legs flung forward as he was sucked through. The next instant, the bull's-eye was once again a static ripple of solid glass.

The tower went silent except for the wind wailing outside and beating against the gallery windows. And then the gears groaned as the lens began to swivel once more, the beams of light sweeping out to sea as if everything were perfectly normal.

Griffin tried to scream, but all that came out was a whine of trapped air. His muscles weren't working right. His knees collapsed, and he slumped forward.

Sykes released him, deadweight, and Griffin slid to the ground. He crawled up the stairs, hoisting himself upright when he reached the top. He stumbled around the lens, banging his fists against the glass, but nothing gave.

"Dad!" he shrieked.

But Philip was gone. He was just—gone.

Griffin tripped and crashed to the ground. Rain splattered against the newly washed windows, tracing down the glass and scarring the sky. Griffin curled into himself, shaking off the hands that tried to lift him away. He pressed his face into the cold steel floor and wailed right along with the wind.

TIME FOR BED, SWEET BOY. WHAT'S THAT—YOU WANT A story first?

All right, then. Under the covers you go.

Listen while I tell you about the world of dreams. At least, that's what it used to be.

I want you to close your eyes and imagine a world with a lighthouse just like this one, but everything else is different. Take away the ocean and the beach and all the spruce and ferns covering the headland behind us. Instead, the ground on this world stretches out from the lighthouse all the way to the horizon, broken only by clusters of homes and stands of wide-leaved trees.

High in the canopy the trees collect clouds—so many they block out the sun and the moon. They cover the whole sky, merry and plump, filled to bursting with dreams.

For generations, while the people of Somni slept at night, the stuff of dreams left their bodies with each exhale, rising up to fill the clouds. The clouds in turn fed the trees, cooling their leaves and shading their branches. And the trees produced air to breathe, as all trees do—but with one big difference. Breathing this air was like inhaling magic. Magic!

The trees and their people lived happily together until one day when the trees began to die. The clouds thinned

Melanie Crowder

without the canopy to tend them, and the air grew stag-
nant and ordinary. The people of Somni tried to save their
beloved trees, but it was too late. Without the clouds, and
without the magic, their minds grew foggy. Their steps
became listless, and they forgot the very thing that might
have saved them.

They forgot to dream.

But you haven't forgotten, have you?

Clever boy. So close your eyes, sweet one, and dream.

5

HEADQUARTERS

THE COLD STEEL of the lantern room floor began to seep into Griffin's skin and shiver through his bones. Every inch of him ached, but when his mind tried to crawl back toward the memory—to the reason for the hurt, the chill would take over again, slowing his breath, his blinking eyes, and his mind.

Through the damp curtain of his eyelashes, Griffin watched the storm keen and thrash outside. He was all alone in the tower. The others had left at some point, given up on the boy who had collapsed in grief. Eventually, there was nothing for Griffin to do but stumble blearily down to the workroom and into the building storm. He hardly noticed when one of the Keepers stepped out from beneath the spiral staircase, following him at a distance. Griffin wove through the forest, raindrops stinging his nose and cheeks and forehead. *Wake up! Wake up!* they seemed to say. *You'll need your wits about you for what's ahead.*

When Griffin entered the cottage, Dr. Hibbert stood in the dining room like a sea captain on the bridge, surveying her crew. A tall man with hunched shoulders combed through the pantry, peering behind cereal boxes and upending the basket of Pop-Tarts. Another one with huge muscles tossed the cushions off the sitting room sofa and shook out the pages of each book on the shelf, the spines creaking in protest.

"Don't forget to search Philip's room. The book is small—it could have fallen behind the bedside table or beneath the mattress." Dr. Hibbert turned to consider Griffin. "I suppose we'll have to take you with us. Go pack an overnight bag. We're leaving for headquarters in five minutes."

Griffin lumbered upstairs, still reeling. He tossed his Tevas, a hoodie, pajamas, and a toothbrush into his backpack and slumped onto his bed. *"He's gone."* The words spilled out of Griffin's mouth, but he couldn't seem to grasp what they meant.

On the wall opposite the bed, his mother's drawings stared back at him. The sketch of Dr. Hibbert. The pen-and-ink diagram of the Fresnel lens. The pastel landscape of the sun setting on the water, with the three Fenns huddled together in the sand, watching for the last flicker of light.

Griffin swallowed a sob. He crossed the room and carefully removed every one of his mother's drawings. He wasn't going anywhere without them. He shuffled the papers together and wrapped them around the journal, tucking them safely inside the pouch at his waist.

You know more than you think you do.

That's what his father had said. But Griffin could barely make one thought connect to the next. It hurt too much to remember what had happened back there, in the tower. And what did he know, anyway? When it came to people being sucked into what was supposed to be solid glass? Nothing. He didn't know a single thing.

"We're leaving," Dr. Hibbert called up the stairs.

Griffin backed out of his bedroom. He took one last look at the blank wall, at the stack of books due back at the library any day, at the door to his father's empty room. None of this was how it was supposed to be. He kept casting around himself as if he were forgetting something. But of course, it was no *thing* he was missing, and no amount of rummaging through drawers or checking under furniture would bring back what he had lost. Griffin trudged downstairs.

Under any other circumstances, a ride in that big orange helicopter would have made his week. But as it was, Griffin barely registered being hefted inside and strapped to his seat. If his stomach lurched when the helicopter lifted off the ground, he hardly noticed. And he didn't glance once at the angry clouds to the west, the silver-tipped waves, or the coastline that swayed in hollows and peaks below.

Instead, his mind played over and over again the terrible moment when his father had disappeared. He was right there, and then he was gone. Griffin squeezed his eyes shut. He barely breathed. His heart thudded slowly, too slowly, inside his chest.

This couldn't be happening.

The inside of the helicopter was freezing, even though it was crammed with people. Now that there was nothing left to do but sit and wait until they reached headquarters (whatever that meant), the shock of it all hit Griffin like a broadside wave slapping across his cheek. He began to shiver, his teeth rattling and his knees knocking together.

Since his mother's funeral, Griffin had rarely been away from his father's side. There had been people, of course, who had declared that the boy should have returned to school. But Griffin, terrified of being away from the only parent he had left, had clung to his dad, refusing to leave. Lost in his own grief, Philip had relented and homeschooled his son. Over the years, the two had settled into their little routines, and eventually, never being farther apart than the reach of a walkie-talkie came to seem almost normal. They had been happy—as much as people living lives two-thirds full could be.

But one-third full? How could a person even make it through a single day?

The pitch of the rotors beating the air dropped, and the helicopter swung inland, hovering over a tall concrete building hidden in a stand of even taller evergreens. Half of the roof was a glass dome, and the other half was flat, with a broad *H* painted in the center. When the helicopter landed, the engine stalled, the blades slowed, and the doors slid open. Fat raindrops pinged shin high off the roof as one by one the grown-ups jumped out and hurried over to the door jutting out of the roof.

Griffin followed them inside and down three flights of stairs that descended snug against the broad exterior walls, leaving the center of the lofty entryway open. Windows cut into stone alcoves at each landing let in a muted light. On the ground floor, an atrium like you'd find in a science museum burst with life, a trio of skinny trees reaching almost to the domed glass ceiling. Ferns and lichens sprouted from the moist branches, and a songbird alighted between fronds. The air was thicker, somehow, in the canopy, almost like a trapped cloud.

Griffin moved to the banister and reached out his hand, brushing the tips of the cone-and-needle branches. He frowned as a memory flitted by so quickly he nearly missed it. It tugged at him—the trees and their companion cloud—but he couldn't quite catch it.

"Don't dawdle," Dr. Hibbert called over her shoulder.

When Griffin reached the ground floor, everyone else had already disappeared through the big wooden doors across the atrium. He took a moment to breathe in the smell of the rich soil, and he tilted his chin up for a dizzying view of the canopy. The room was a little like being in the woods behind the lighthouse. If he closed his eyes, he could almost convince himself that he could hear the waves crashing onto the beach below, his dad right there beside him.

Dr. Hibbert considered the boy in front of her, dripping with rainwater that pooled on the concrete floor beneath his feet. It wasn't an easy thing to look someone so clearly devastated square in the face. And Hypatia Hibbert wasn't accustomed to dealing with children. Griffin was the first to ever enter the Keepers' headquarters, and she didn't have a clue what to do with him.

"Won't you sit?" she asked, indicating a row of high-backed chairs along the far wall.

Griffin shook his head.

"Would you like to take off your raincoat?"

Griffin tugged the zipper up over his chin.

Dr. Hibbert's jaw ticked to the side. "I'm not the bad guy here."

Griffin still didn't answer. He was having a difficult time keeping any of her words inside his head long enough for them to drop anchor. Her questions mostly drifted by like severed floats bobbing on the outgoing tide.

Dr. Hibbert sighed, a long, drawn-out sort of sigh meant to make anyone within earshot aware of her exasperation. "Young man, we have a common enemy. You are not mine, and I am certainly not yours."

Griffin blinked, trying to focus on her words. "What do you mean? What enemy?"

Dr. Hibbert clicked her tongue. "I'm not sure I should tell you that."

"What? Why not?"

"If your parents wanted you to know that information, they would have told you themselves."

Griffin reeled as if she had slapped him across the face. He wasn't ready to hear his dad talked about like that—like something from the past. He'd only just gotten used to thinking of his mother that way. So he slapped back, before the blow took the wind out of him. "If you know something about what happened to my dad and you're not telling me—"

Dr. Hibbert waved him off. "Your parents trusted me to lead the Keepers; I can't think of a single reason why you should feel any differently."

Griffin rocked back on his heels. *The Keepers?* That was the phrase his dad had used. "Keepers of what?"

"The Society of Lighthouse Keepers, of course."

Griffin crossed his arms over his chest. "Lighthouse keepers wash windows and polish lenses. *We* do that. Me and my dad. But this 'headquarters' is— what, five miles inland? You're not anywhere close to the water. So what is it, *exactly*, that your society does?"

Dr. Hibbert brushed a wayward hair out of her face, considering her words carefully. "We are a collection of scientists, commissioned by the Coast Guard to . . . *protect* the populace. Our particular expertise hasn't been needed much in the past few years. The lighthouse has been quiet. As I'm sure you've figured out by now, it can be extremely dangerous."

There was truth in what she said. But it wasn't the whole truth; Griffin was sure of that. Griffin eyed the woman who stood before him, rigid as a snag in a forest of downed trees. Her eyes were fixed in a permanent squint, and vertical lines carved into the skin above her lips (perhaps because she was a little too fond of pursing them).

If you look closely when you're working with glass, you can see imperfections, you can feel vulnerabilities. There might be a hairline crack or a bubble trapped inside.

It's not so easy with people.

Griffin squinted, inspecting Dr. Hibbert like he would a piece of freshly annealed glass. "What do my parents have to do with any of this?"

Dr. Hibbert turned to face the trees. "Katherine designed this room. Did you know that? And Philip installed the ceiling. We worked on it together, actually. I'm a botanist, you see. Each Keeper contributes what he or she can. And we have all sacrificed greatly. But our enemy is so much bigger than any one of us and our own private tragedies.

"Anyway, your mother's . . . trips . . . taught her certain things"—Dr. Hibbert gestured upward—"insights she shared with the rest of us."

The memory Griffin hadn't quite been able to

catch earlier snagged a second time. It was of his mother, telling one of her bedtime stories, and though he couldn't remember the words, it warmed him, and it gave him courage.

"*You* sent her on those trips. You're the reason we lost her."

Dr. Hibbert almost hid any start the accusation had given her, but Griffin had been watching, waiting to catch her out in one of those almost truths. There—a stiffening of the fingers, knuckles pressing against the thin fabric of her pockets. You could almost say her hands clenched into fists.

"How do you know about that?" Dr. Hibbert's voice had gone cold and sharp.

"My dad told me things." Griffin tried to sound more confident than he felt. "He tells me everything."

Dr. Hibbert pursed her lips. One eyebrow quirked upward. "I wouldn't be so sure."

The concrete walls sucked her words into their pores. Griffin tried to swallow, but something was getting in the way of the air headed for his lungs.

She turned on her heel, her braid whipping over her shoulder. "I'll send someone to show you to your room. You may as well get comfortable." And with that, Hypatia Hibbert crossed to a tall wooden door set into the opposite wall and swept through it. In the seconds before the door slammed behind her, the sound of agitated conversations, clanking dishes, and hurried footfalls slipped into the quiet atrium.

Griffin glanced around him—at the bare concrete walls and the high security fence outside the window—and began to wonder if he wasn't exactly a guest in this place, but something much more like a prisoner.

6

PERFECTLY IRRATIONAL ANSWERS

ALMOST AS SOON AS Dr. Hibbert left, a second woman emerged. She approached the base of the trees, where Griffin stood in the dirt, leaning against the solid trunks as if they were the only things keeping him upright. Like Dr. Hibbert, this woman also had deep wrinkles stretching across her forehead and braided hair colored by the shock of age. But that was where any resemblance between the two ended.

This woman's white braids curled under her ears, ending in feathery tufts that bobbed in an almost childlike way. "You're Griffin. I'm Beatrix." She seemed to know that he wouldn't want to talk, so she kept on in her lilting voice that hopped between tones for no particular reason. "We've got a room ready for you. If we hit the kitchen on the way up, I'll sneak us a handful of cookies."

Beatrix laid a gentle hand on Griffin's shoulder, and she waited until he was ready to leave the hush of the atrium for the flurry at the rest of headquarters. But Griffin couldn't bring himself to move. Beatrix seemed nice enough, but she worked for Dr. Hibbert. He couldn't trust her.

After Griffin's mother died, trust hadn't come easily. His father had seen this and tried with every action, every day, to say straight to his son's trembling heart: *I am here. I am here. I am here.* But it didn't matter in the end how steady Philip had been. He was gone now too.

Griffin rested his hand on the pouch strapped around his stomach. What he needed was time alone, to think. So when Beatrix once again applied gentle pressure between his shoulder blades, he let that little push propel him forward.

Griffin followed her through the thick wooden door and even thicker walls. Beyond, a wide corridor bisected the first floor. To the left was a kitchen with swinging doors, a narrow dining room, and a flight of floating stairs leading up to a second floor. To the right was a conference room and an enormous library filled with people whispering in flustered groups.

Dr. Hibbert sat at an aluminum desk planted in the middle of a freestanding glass box at the center of it all. Her eyes darted from the paper in her hands to the people busy in the kitchen and hurrying between the library and the conference room and, finally, to where Griffin stood.

He shuddered. The entire building had a stony, modern air, but Dr. Hibbert's office in particular seemed to blow a chill across his cheeks. Beatrix reemerged from the kitchen and steered him up the stairs to a quiet hallway with no fewer than a dozen closed doors. She led him into a small, plain room. It contained exactly four pieces of furniture: a twin bed, a cupboard for clothes, a chair by the door, and a wobbly bedside table.

Beatrix set a tray of food on the chair (as promised, with a teetering pile of molasses cookies) and backed away. "Sleep well, child. I'm right next door if you need anything." And she closed the door softly behind her.

Griffin let out a long sigh. Missing his dad throbbed like a couple of cracked ribs. Even shallow breaths were sharp with pain. But he didn't have time to curl up on the small bed in the corner and let grief crush him.

Nothing that had happened that afternoon made

sense. Griffin moved the chair in front of the door and sat, tipping the seat back in case anyone tried to push the door open. He unfastened the strap around his waist and pulled out his father's journal and his mother's artwork.

Griffin began with the drawings. He sorted them into two piles: one that seemed random and a second that might have anything to do with the lighthouse or Dr. Hibbert and the Keepers. He tucked the first bunch back in the pouch and lifted the small stack that remained, careful not to crease the thin paper or smudge a single one of his mother's lines. He examined the drawings, and sure enough, he noticed things he'd overlooked before.

On an aerial sketch of the big Fresnel lens in the lighthouse, she had written *portal access* in tiny letters that nearly blended in with the grated-metal floor. Griffin's gaze had slid over that sketch several times a day, but he'd never noticed that his mom had also inscribed a name above each of the carefully drawn bull's-eyes. First *Earth*, then *Caligo, Stella, Arida*, and *Glac*— The rest of the word was lost as it followed the angled panels out of sight.

Griffin frowned. Portal access? What did that even mean?

He placed the paper on his lap and picked up the

next one. It was a colored-pencil drawing of the light-house tower, only the small workroom attached to the base was missing. In its place was the cross section of what looked like a huge temple. All through the nave were narrow alcoves fit with breathing masks and webs of tubing. His mother's careful script noted the dimensions of each niche in the wall and the path the tubes took to vent in the tower high above.

Outside the temple was an amphitheater; beyond that, barracks and a narrow rectangular building labeled *rectory*. The rooms inside were all marked: *priests' bedrooms, offices, guard stations*. At the heart of the building was an eight-sided space labeled *chapel*.

Griffin frowned. Why would his mom draw the lighthouse tower on top of a temple? And why had she gone to such lengths to note all those details about a place that was just in her imagination?

Beams of light radiated from the tower—at least he'd always thought that's what those squiggly lines were supposed to be. And they were, but as Griffin peered closer, he realized they were also more of his mom's careful handwriting.

The traveler must center himself in front of the bull's-eye, stall the gears, and

focus all his want on that singular world.
If the need is great enough, the glass will
respond. But be wary of standing so close;
another's desire on the other side can
draw the unsuspecting through.

There was more, but Griffin would need a magnifying glass to read it—something about stolen dreamers and worlds taken in conquest.

Wait—*worlds*? Griffin sat back in surprise. Not, like, traveling around the globe, but from one world to another? His mom couldn't possibly mean that. Could she?

All of a sudden, missing her rose up into his throat, as if everything he hadn't been able to say to her over the past three years was lodged there, trying to find its way into words all at once. His mom *would* have meant traveling between worlds. That's exactly the kind of impossible idea she would've whispered over his head while he drifted off to sleep.

Griffin ran his fingers over her words. A portal? Hope squeezed his lungs, made his breaths come quick and hard. A portal isn't a dead end. It leads somewhere, right? So where, then? And did that mean his dad was somewhere else? Not dead, just on the other side of a portal between worlds?

Melanie Crowder

48

Griffin had watched him get sucked through that lens. *Through the portal,* he corrected himself. One minute he was right there, and the next he was gone. Griffin squeezed his eyes shut. It was impossible. Wasn't it?

Griffin turned to the following page. It showed a pastel sketch of the exact clothes the Keepers had all worn—pajama-like things cropped at the knee and elbow, with a red sash around the waist. A swatch of pale blue fabric was stapled to the paper—it was breathable and soft, like well-worn linen. Something about it was different, though. Griffin rubbed the cloth between his fingers. He pulled it first one way and then the other. It stretched out and sprang back, but there weren't any crisscrossing fibers like you'd find in a swatch of cotton or denim, or anything else on Earth for that matter.

The last page was a watercolor of a cavern filled with trees, just like in the atrium. But the trees weren't like any Griffin had ever seen before. They were as tall as redwoods with broad fanlike leaves you'd find in the tropics. Notes on soil, light, and cloud cultivation in the canopy filled the margins.

Griffin set that page on top of the others. Reality and memory collided, blurring the edges of his vision and overlaying everything in sepia. He'd seen those

The Lighthouse between the Worlds

trees before. Not in the drawings on his wall, not in the botanic gardens in Portland, but in his mind. His mother had been sitting on the edge of his bed, tucking the covers up under his chin and telling him a bedtime story.

Wait. Had his mom *been* to those other worlds? Had she seen them with her own eyes, breathed in the dream clouds on Somni and traipsed through the jungle of Vinea? The tips of Griffin's fingers began to tingle, and then his toes, like when you roll over in the middle of the night to find that your limbs are dead asleep. But you shake them, no matter how much it burns, until they wake up.

Questions Griffin didn't even know he'd been living with all those years sidled next to perfectly irrational answers. A portal to other worlds. Right there, in his lighthouse.

If his mom had traveled to those other worlds, or even just one of them, maybe he could too. Maybe he could go find his dad and bring him back home. Griffin raked his fingers through his hair. The day before, he and his dad had ground a bevel into a round of glass just like the concentric circles in the lens, to catch the light, his dad had said. But what if it was more than that? What if his dad had been trying to teach him something about the portal without freaking him out? What if both of them were trying to tell Griffin something—through his lessons, through her stories and sketches—dropping clues for him to pick up later?

It was all too much. The journal and all the papers slid to the floor as Griffin dropped his head into his hands. Tears pricked his eyes. His nose ran and his ears rang and his chest was one steady ache. Rain drummed into the roof overhead, and the four walls of the tiny room muffled the sounds within. There are some things no one else has any right to hear.

Gradually, clanking dishes and a phone that nobody seemed to care to answer ringing on the floor below brought Griffin back to himself. He drew his sleeve across his nose and wiped his hands off on his jeans. He had work to do. It was too late for his mom, but he could still do something about his dad. He *had* to do something, and soon.

Griffin plucked the journal off the floor and opened it. To anyone else, the notes that filled each page would have seemed like gibberish, but he recognized the shorthand immediately. He swiped at the edges of his eyes and flipped through the small book, front to back. All the bits and pieces tumbled together like bubbles of air in a cresting wave. The pictures may have been a puzzle, but he knew exactly what this was.

No two pieces of glass are the same. Of course, factories these days can get it pretty close. But any number of variables alter the composition: thickness, coloring agents, or the ratio of silica and soda, lime and lead. Those differences subtly change the way the light moves through the pane, whether it is caught and redirected, channeled, or diffused. And that doesn't even begin to take into account curved or etched glass, impurities, or plain-old mistakes.

Every day, in the family glass studio, Philip would jot a recipe of sorts onto the chalkboard to specify the color and weight of the glass they'd be working with that day. The angle and precise measurements of the mold or carving—it would all be there, in the shorthand that had become like a second language between them.

The journal was simple. There were eight sections with a bull's-eye sketched at the beginning of each one and what were becoming familiar names written above: Earth, Caligo, Stella, Arida, Glacies, Maris, Somni, and Vinea. The following pages were filled with glassmakers' notes. To the untrained eye, the drawings looked identical. But Griffin knew better. He could see irregularities in the concentric circles that made up each panel of glass and read them in the notes scrawled across the pages. Each bull's-eye was different, the impurities and subtle variations a map charting the way to a particular world.

Everything around Griffin ground to a stop. His breathing. His heartbeat. *This was it.* The portal wasn't some mystery he'd never understand. It was glass.

Griffin scrambled to pick up his mother's drawings. He could do this. He could. He wrapped the drawings carefully around the journal once more and tucked them into the pouch at his waist. He stood and dragged the chair away from the door. He kicked his shoes off and climbed into bed. His dad was right. Griffin did know more than he'd realized. Maybe he even knew enough to bring his dad home.

MURDERERS

UNLIKE THE FOGHORN or the tsunami siren, there are some noises you don't even notice until they stop. Like when the electricity shorts, and suddenly the hum of the refrigerator and the low roar of the furnace quit. Or at the end of a ferry ride when the engine gears down and you can hear the waves slapping against the hull. Griffin had been so lost in thought he hadn't noticed the hallway outside his door rumbling all evening with the steady patter of people hurrying back and forth. But then it all went quiet.

Griffin hopped out of bed, pressed his ear against the door, and listened. On the ground floor of head-quarters, chair legs scraped against the concrete. He eased his door open. The hall was empty. Moonlight yawned out of windows set high in the thick walls.

Griffin crept out of his room, his bare feet slapping against the hardwood floor, and down the staircase. He didn't see anyone in the wide corridor or in Dr. Hibbert's glass office. He peeked through the porthole window into the kitchen, where a teetering stack of dinner dishes had been left to soak in the deep aluminum sink.

A buzz of voices in the conference room floated across the still air. Griffin snuck over to the library. Bookshelves covered the wall to his left, and a bank of filing cabinets lined the one on his right. In a gap between shelves, down by the floor, an embellished grate covered one of the building's air vents. Dappled light and muffled voices from the room next door filtered through. Griffin crouched low, his breath held tight in his chest, and he listened.

All the Keepers were packed inside. And every single one of them was arguing.

"I thought you said you handled this! You said they would leave us alone!"

"We should pull apart that lens piece by piece so they can't come back ever again."

"Philip already tried that, remember? It doesn't work."

"We don't have time to waste arguing—Somni

could be gathering those priests with their creepy mind control and preparing to cross a whole army of soldiers over."

Griffin sat back, stunned. An army?

There are a dozen reasons why it's risky to swim in the water off the Oregon coast. Submerged logs tumble through the surf. The ocean floor is dotted with hidden rocks that will pull a swimmer under and pin him there. And then there are the sharks, of course. But the most dangerous thing? Rip currents.

You don't even know you've been caught up in the rush of water speeding out to the open ocean before you're too far gone to call for help. You're treading water, but the waves are only getting bigger, and you know you're not strong enough to fight the current back to shore.

Griffin gulped for air, lifting his chin high as if he were struggling to keep his head above water. What could he possibly do against a whole army?

The voices in the conference room rose to shouts, swelling and raging to drown their fear. Griffin leaned forward again, pressing his ear to the grate.

"What we need to do is call in the Coast Guard. We can't handle a full-scale invasion on our own."

"But we still don't know what changed! They left us alone for three years. We need to know why—"

"We're never going to know enough."

"We need to find Philip's notes!"

"Are you kidding? They just kidnapped Philip. It won't be long before the priests make him tell them what Katherine did to the lens."

The man kept talking, but the words turned fuzzy until they were a tinny ringing in Griffin's ears. *Kidnapped.* His dad hadn't just disappeared, then. Someone had taken him. Someone who could move between worlds, with armies at the ready.

There were other worlds out there. And his dad was on one of them. Alone. Maybe hurt. Probably afraid. Griffin pressed his palms against his temples and squeezed.

Gradually, voices from the conference room slipped back in the lull between waves of panic rolling over Griffin.

"*We* don't even know what Katherine did to the lens. If Philip didn't tell *us*, then he's definitely not going to—"

"Enough!" Dr. Hibbert's stern voice cut through the rest, and the bickering around the conference table grumbled and fell silent. "I sent a crew to sweep the cottage for Philip's book. If they don't find it by morning, we'll have to admit that it's lost to us for good."

Griffin frowned. Was she talking about his dad's journal?

"Clearly Somni is tampering with the lens. By taking even one of us through the portal, they've broken our agreement." An undercurrent of long-simmering rage filled her voice. "Tomorrow we'll send a team to the lighthouse at sunset. Fergus, Sykes, and I will travel to Somni to see what we can learn. The rest of the team will remain at the lighthouse, standing guard in case anyone comes through while we're gone."

Dr. Hibbert paused, daring anyone to disagree with her. "We're left with two options. Either we find a way to repair the block Katherine put on the lens, or we have to cut the tether between Earth and Somni, closing the portal for good. The block must have failed, and with Philip gone and his notebook with him, we don't have a glassmaker to solve that particular puzzle for us. That leaves us with no choice. We must sever any human link between the two worlds."

All around the conference table, the Keepers erupted in protest.

"You know what we stand to lose if we don't!" Dr. Hibbert's voice cracked as she shouted to regain control. The others quieted, and she continued softly, though the hard edge remained. "This is the last thing any of us wants. But are you willing to gamble everyone on Earth for the sake of a few lives?"

This time the Keepers stayed silent, as if they didn't dare breathe.

"Tomorrow at sunset—during our limited window of time when the Somni side will be unguarded—we'll open the portal. If we can't bring every last dreamer from Earth home with us, they have to be sacrificed, right there in the temple."

Griffin backed away in horror. Footsteps scraped against the concrete floor in the next room. He hurried out of the library, ducking into the kitchen just as the door from the conference room creaked open. Griffin cast around for somewhere to hide, then scurried under the sink, pulling shut the curtains that hid a tangle of pipes and drip pans from sight.

Someone approached the kitchen. The door swung open. Griffin held his breath until he thought he was going to explode. Booted feet clomped across the tile, paused at the opposite swinging door, and pushed through into the dining room. Griffin counted to ten before wiggling free of the pipes and pans, then he tiptoed out the door and up the stairs back to his room. He slipped under the covers and squeezed his eyes shut.

Murderers.

Griffin's heart hammered against his chest, so loud it seemed like they must be able to hear it all the way down in the conference room. The Keepers weren't scientists or researchers or any of that nonsense Dr. Hibbert had said before. They were murderers. They were going to kill all the people from Earth that Somni had stolen. They were going to kill his dad.

The door to Griffin's room eased open. He wanted to scream. He wanted to ball his hands into fists and pummel whoever it was, make him hurt half as much as he did. But when you're a kid in a world of grownups, you can't just do what you want, not when they hold all the power.

So though Griffin's head throbbed and his heart ached, he kept his eyes closed, and he willed his body still. A dagger of light lanced across his cheek, and he felt someone cross the room and lean over him, watching for any movement. With a quiet *hmph*, the person left, closing the door. Griffin's eyes snapped open. He rolled onto his back, and his hand rose to his chest.

Griffin had read more books in his eleven years than most grown-ups. He and his father had gone to the library at least three times a week to swap out one stack for another. He'd read books about parasites and tornados, quicksand and every kind of shark. Griffin thought if he read enough about scary things (especially the sort that could steal a parent away) he'd shake the feeling that any day he was going to lose his dad, just like he'd already lost his mom. Or if that didn't work, at least he'd be prepared.

The night after he'd read a book about clogged arteries, cardiac arrest, and open-heart surgery, he'd lain flat on his back, probing the long, ridged bone that ran down his chest and wondering what it must be like to have your chest cracked wide open.

Well, he didn't have to wonder anymore. In that moment, Griffin knew exactly how it must feel.

The Keepers were going to open the portal the following night. And they were going through to— where did they say? Somni? Then, when they got to the other side, they were going to kill every last person from Earth.

They were going to kill his dad.

———————————— ≋ • ≋ ————————————

IT'S TIME FOR BED, SWEET GRIFFIN.

What's that? You don't want another story about a made-up world?

You think it's all nonsense? Hmmm.

I'll tell you what. You try, just this once, to set your suspicions aside, and I'll tell you the story of how all those worlds came to be.

Deal?

Okay, then. Snuggle up.

Long ago, a starburst of energy bloomed in the sky like a many-petaled flower, and Earth was born, along with seven other worlds. They spun together for millions of years, waiting for a way between them to open.

In the beginning, each world was a perfect copy of the next, and they seemed identical until the great melt. Some, like Glacies, have yet to emerge from an ice age. Others, like Arida, warmed far too quickly.

The humans who inhabited each world evolved differently to suit their home. To adapt to the skies of Caligo, the people's bones thinned until they were hollow as a bird's. On Stella, it was their eyes that changed until, like owls, they could see in the dark as well as you and I do in the daylight. If the sjel trees hadn't died, interrupting the dream cycle, in another generation or two, the people of

Somni might not have spoken at all and would have communicated only with their minds.

A way between worlds finally opened 124 years ago, when the first beam shone out of our lighthouse. The glassmaker had only meant to construct a beacon to guide the ships at sea. He couldn't have known the magic that moved beneath his fingers, how the want *of the eight worlds would shift the glass, shaping it to meet that need.*

When the glassmaker first switched the light on and the lens began to turn, a great tremor coursed through the sky. The creatures of each world felt the change in their bones, and they welcomed it.

You think I'm teasing? No—I swear to you: It's true.

The eight worlds were always meant to be connected. We need one another, Griffin. We are so much stronger together.

8

BETTER FORGOTTEN

WHEN YOU'RE UP in the lighthouse tower at night, and you look out the floor-to-ceiling windows, all you see is shadows: the restless dark of the sea and the jagged pitch of treetops outlining the headland behind you. The beams swivel across the land and the ocean, and anyone could spot you up there in the tower, the bright light illuminating your every feature, but you'd never even know they watched from the darkness below.

When he walked into the dining room for breakfast the following morning, Griffin felt that same shiver of exposure. He stopped still at the entrance, sure everyone in headquarters was staring at him. He hadn't slept much the night before. Every time he almost drifted off, he'd remember that his dad was in danger. His eyes would fly open again, and that same chest-cracking ache would settle in.

Griffin crossed to the buffet table. There weren't any Pop-Tarts or cinnamon squares, just a bunch of heart-healthy options. He sighed, scooped three lumps of oatmeal into a bowl, and sprinkled a hefty portion of brown sugar over the top. He grabbed a bottle of orange juice and looked around for a place to sit. Fergus and Sykes watched him from the middle of the long table down the center of the room. Fergus wore a blazer that was at least two sizes too small (probably to make his muscles look even bigger than they already were). He had the kind of bushy eyebrows that barely left a gap between them. Sykes, on the other hand, was tall and lean. He hunched over his buttered pumpernickel toast, knobby elbows splayed wide like he thought someone was going to try to snatch it out of his hands at any moment. Griffin skittered around the outside of the dining room, as far away from those two as he could get.

In the corner, Beatrix sat at a round café table. She was a tiny woman, but she waved over her head and beamed so enthusiastically that she was impossible to miss.

"And how did you sleep?" she asked when Griffin took the seat opposite her.

"Oh—um, great. My bed is super comfy. I didn't wake up once." Griffin ducked his head and shoved a spoonful of oatmeal into his mouth.

"I'm glad to hear that. It's not always easy sleeping in a new place."

Griffin darted a look around the dining room. Everybody was dressed for a chilly day, in jeans or khakis and sweaters or thick long-sleeved shirts. There was no idle conversation. No friendly banter. And hardly anyone was making eye contact.

Good, Griffin thought. *You should feel guilty.* But then he froze. A blob of oatmeal slid off his spoon and plopped back into the bowl.

"Beatrix?"

"Yes, dear?"

"Everybody is in normal clothes today."

The elderly woman tilted her head to the side, perplexed.

"Yesterday everyone was wearing the same pajama things."

"Ah," Beatrix said with a fluttering laugh. "You mean the stola?"

"The what?"

"The blue pants and shirt, with the red sash. It's called a stola. Keepers are given a set at their induction ceremony."

"Then, yeah, the stola. Why did everybody have them on yesterday but not today?"

"Oh!" Beatrix's whole face brightened. "They'll have them on again this evening. They only wear the stola when they have good reason to."

Like when they're traveling to a different world? Griffin glanced down at his raincoat and jeans. Was that why the Keepers had all worn stolas the day before? Because when the alarm sounded, they assumed they'd be going through the portal? They must have been dressed to blend in once they got there.

"They? But aren't you a Keeper too?"

"Oh, yes," Beatrix said cheerily enough before her face fell. "But they don't ask me to wear the stola anymore. I'm only here for my brain, you know. They don't need me for . . . trips. Just the physics. And anyway, I'm not sure I'd want to go. . . ." She trailed off, her cloudy eyes losing their focus.

"Go where?" Griffin barely breathed. He wanted so badly to understand what was going on. And it almost seemed like she might answer whatever he asked, in the middle of breakfast. Right under Dr. Hibbert's nose. "How are those trips even possible?"

But Beatrix didn't seem to hear his questions. Her mind was somewhere else entirely. She blinked slowly, her eyelashes meeting like a moth drying its wings. After a long moment, her eyes settled again on Griffin's puzzled face. She stretched across the table and patted his hand.

"Some memories are better forgotten."

Griffin squirmed. He didn't like the sound of that. If Beatrix had been there—to Somni—and never wanted to return, it didn't sound like a good place. At all.

And then an idea struck. Beatrix had *been* there. She would have a stola, a set she probably never even bothered to put on anymore. Griffin shoveled the rest of his oatmeal into his mouth, tightened the cap on his juice, and leaped up from his chair. "I gotta go. Sorry."

He scurried out of the dining room, nearly crashing into Dr. Hibbert as he pushed through the swinging door into the corridor. Oily black coffee sloshed inside her mug, and she stepped back, holding the mug as far away from her crisp white blazer as she could reach. Griffin skirted around her, and she let him pass, her eyebrows raised and her lips twisted at a distinctly suspicious angle.

"I, uh—forgot something in my room."

Griffin darted upstairs and flung open his door. He'd never been what you'd call a neat child. You'd never find his shoes lined up by the door or his coats all on the proper hangers or hooks. He preferred things a little messy. But as with most messy people, it was *his* mess, and it was just the way he liked it. So when he took in the rumpled sheets and the clothes strewn over the floor, he knew, through to his bones, that someone had been in there, rifling through his stuff.

If somebody had gone to the trouble to ransack his room, that meant the Keepers had guessed he was hiding something. Griffin rested a hand on the front pocket of his hoodie, trying to shake the uneasy feeling that had crept over him. Beneath the layers of bulky cotton, the journal and the drawings were safe, strapped around his waist.

Griffin squared his shoulders. His mouth set in a stubborn line. They didn't know everything. He ducked into Beatrix's room next door, heading straight for the clothes cupboard. He didn't have the luxury of flinging everything all over the place—Beatrix was a tidy one. So he pulled out each stack of clothes and carefully thumbed through them. Shoved at the very back of the cupboard, behind a tower of thick woolen sweaters, was her stola, the red sash wrapped reverently around the soft fabric. Beneath the stola was a pair of worn sandals. Griffin held them up against the soles of his boots. They were several sizes too small. He set them back on the shelf; his Tevas would have to do. Griffin closed the wardrobe and stuffed the bundle under his hoodie. He dashed out into the hallway and back to his room.

A crooked smile drifted across his lips. He peeled off the layers of his own clothes and lifted the blue shirt over his head. It was loose, but not horribly so. He stepped into the pants. Those he had to hold up with one hand while he wrapped and tied the sash around his waist like a belt.

Griffin pulled his jeans and hoodie over the gauzy fabric. They were a little more snug than usual, but if he wore his raincoat on top of it all, he didn't think anyone would notice. His Tevas were going to look funny—nobody wore sandals in this kind of weather. But hopefully no one would be looking at his feet.

Griffin blew out a long breath, and the worst jangling of his nerves left with it. He was as ready as he was going to get. He could do this. He could.

Now he just had to find out a way out of there.

9

STOWAWAY

IN THE MOVIES, the bad guys always seem to be shoving somebody into the trunk of a car and speeding off to do whatever nefarious deeds bad guys do. But nobody would ever put *himself* in the trunk of that car to be driven off with—would he?

If Griffin had been any less desperate, he'd never even have considered it. But he'd already tried every other option. He'd waited behind a bush by the electronic gate for hours, hoping someone would drive through so he could slip out and away. He'd gone for a walk on the grounds looking for a place to jump the fence, only the towering steel structure was too high. He'd thought if he could just get out, then maybe he could run all the way home, or at least to the coast highway. Once he got that far, he could always hitchhike the rest of the way. Or he could wait at one of the scenic viewpoints along the highway where the tourists always pull off to snap pictures. While they were busy reading the signs about sneaker waves or tide pools, he could slip in between crates on those cargo haulers hitched to the back of the RVs. But what if he picked the one rig that didn't stop at the lighthouse and he ended up all the way down in California?

Out of ideas, Griffin trudged back into headquarters, aiming for a dim corner of the library where at least he could think through how to get the portal open once he finally got to the lighthouse, and where, in case anyone had noticed his absence, he could pretend he'd been stuck in a book all day. But the moment he entered the main corridor, Dr. Hibbert swept out of her office. "Went for a walk, did we?"

"Um. Yeah?" Griffin scuffed his Tevas against the concrete.

"Follow me," she ordered, striding back into her office.

Griffin had never thought of glass as cold. To him it was alive. Every piece had a story to tell. But the thick panes that made up the four walls of Dr. Hibbert's office were every bit as frosty as she was, without even a hint of the bending and flexing, of the fire that had birthed it.

Her aluminum desk was bare except for a box with a round speaker set into the top. Dr. Hibbert pushed the red button at the base. "Sykes," she said, and then she lifted her finger, waiting.

A voice crackled through the speaker. "Yes, Dr. Hibbert?"

"Bring two plates into my office, and keep everyone away. I have an important guest." She released the button for the second time and steepled her fingers on the desk, a practiced smile curving over her lips. "So, Griffin, how are you getting along so far?"

Griffin shrugged, glancing back at the door and wishing somebody—anybody—would give him a reason to get out of there. He did not want to sit and eat a friendly meal across from somebody planning to murder his dad. But he'd already skipped lunch, and his stomach was rumbling so loud he knew Dr. Hibbert could hear it.

Her smile didn't crack, and she seemed prepared to wait an eternity for Griffin to remember his manners and answer her question. And she might have, too, if Sykes hadn't pushed through the glass door, ducking his head and balancing a tray in his hands.

With a flourish, he spread a cloth over the aluminum desk and set out brimming plates, silverware, and glasses full of iced tea that looked like it had steeped too long. Sykes backed out of the room (an awkward thing for someone so tall), and then he turned away from the glass wall, standing guard outside the door.

The fake smile reappeared as Dr. Hibbert dropped her napkin into her lap. She seemed to be exerting a great deal of effort to hide her irritation. "What fun— growing up at a lighthouse!" She speared the braised chicken thigh on her plate and drew her knife across the meat in a sawing motion.

Griffin gulped. "I guess so."

"Those vicious winter storms, the beach all to yourself, and that charming little cottage—what an adventure you must have had!"

Griffin stuck a forkful of Tater Tots into his mouth so he wouldn't have to answer right away. "Sure," he finally offered.

"And did you go to school?"

"At home."

Her eyes narrowed, just the tiniest bit at the corners. "I suppose your father taught you all about the lighthouse in the course of your studies?"

Griffin shifted in his chair. He stuffed a heaping

mound of macaroni into his mouth and puffed his cheeks out extra big.

Dr. Hibbert flicked bits of arugula around her plate with the prongs of her fork. "Because if your father told you something—about what he was planning to do with the lens back there—I would hope you'd tell me."

"I don't know anything," Griffin said around his mouthful of food.

Dr. Hibbert's fork gave up flicking and started stabbing. "I thought your father told you everything?"

Griffin squirmed in his chair.

"Well," she said. "If you should remember something, I know you'll come tell me right away. We want to bring your father home, Griffin. And I'd hate to think you knew of a way for us to help him and kept it to yourself. . . ."

She didn't say anything more for the rest of the meal, but she watched him from beneath hooded eyes. Griffin downed the food on his plate as quickly as he could and scurried out of there.

By the time he got back outside, the sun brushed the tips of the cedar trees, already on its way down for the evening. Griffin turned in a frantic circle on the gravel drive. He was out of time. Even if he managed to slip away, he'd never make it to the lighthouse on foot before sunset. And he *had* to beat the Keepers there.

He didn't like it one bit, but Griffin's only option was to somehow sneak onto the Keepers' transport to the lighthouse. The helicopter was long gone, so they had to be driving back. He ducked behind an overly exuberant hydrangea bush beside the front door and waited.

Sure enough, shortly after six o'clock, a caravan of black sedans and a passenger van circled in the packed gravel driveway. The van was quickly loaded with duffel bags, then the drivers disappeared into headquarters. Griffin waited a couple of minutes, and then a few more just to be sure. He crept out onto the driveway and approached the back doors to the van. Inside, the duffel bags were piled up as high as the back seat.

He eyed the sturdy zippers. Maybe he could wiggle himself inside one of those. But what if the zipper stuck and he couldn't get back out again? What if he couldn't breathe in there?

Griffin scraped a fingernail against the thick canvas. He unzipped one of the long zippers and peered inside. The duffel bag wasn't filled with clothes, or food, or even weapons, as he'd imagined. Instead, four stout aluminum canisters were wedged inside. Something was written on the label—Griffin glanced behind him, then swiveled the closest canister until the writing came into full view.

Silica.

He frowned. Why on earth were the Keepers taking silica through the portal? Were there glassmakers on the other side? Griffin zipped the duffel bag back up, snuck around to the passenger side, and eased the door open. In the way back, under the last row of bench seats, was a narrow space he could probably squeeze into. But how long would he be waiting? And what if he was wrong, and the van wasn't headed to the lighthouse at all?

Just then, the front doors to headquarters groaned open. Griffin didn't have another second to decide. He jumped into the van and pulled the door closed behind him. While footsteps crunched across the gravel drive, he scurried to the back row and wedged himself under the seat, scooting as far into the corner as he could get. The instant he pulled his knees up to his chest, the doors opened. The van wobbled and dipped under the weight of the bodies clambering inside and scooting across the bench seats to make room for more people to pile in.

"That's all of us," Fergus announced.

A pair of smelly feet in old leather sandals settled directly in front of Griffin's face. The doors slammed, and the engine turned over. Griffin curled up as tight as he could while the van bumped and swerved. After ten minutes or so, the ride leveled out and the van picked up speed—they must have turned onto the coast highway.

Griffin closed his eyes, hugged his arms over his stomach, and tried to slow his racing mind. But it was no good. He kept picturing his dad tied up on some strange world, with no one there to help him. And really—even if Griffin somehow beat the Keepers up the lighthouse stairs, he still didn't know how to open the portal. He had clues and hunches. But what he needed was more answers. The last thing he wanted to do was lie there and wait.

There's a spot just north of the lighthouse called Devil's Churn. It used to be an underwater cave until wave after crashing wave, year after thousands of years, collapsed the roof overhead. Now it's a narrow inlet you can spot from the highway above. The waves still roar in, and the pressure of all that water rushing through the skinny space is too much sometimes. The water explodes upward, hundreds of feet into the air, where it finds a release at last. Griffin felt exactly like one of those fitful waves, hemmed and penned in when all he wanted was to burst free.

After thirty long minutes, the van slowed, turning in a wide circle before rolling to a stop. "Everybody out," Fergus said. "Hibbert's already at the cottage."

Griffin held his breath while the Keepers filed out of the van. The doors slammed and he waited, cringing, for someone to open the back, yank the luggage out, and spot his hiding place.

But the minutes dragged by, and the chatter faded. Griffin crawled from under the seat and peered out the window. The driveway was empty. He crept to the door and eased outside. His legs tingled as he dropped onto the asphalt. Griffin shook out his arms and banged on his thighs to wake them up.

He was home. Part of him wanted to go inside the little cottage, run straight up to his room, hide under the covers, and pretend like none of this was happening. But it wouldn't feel a bit like home if his dad wasn't there.

The sun wavered above the clouds that hunkered down on the horizon. From its point on the headland, the lighthouse beckoned, the lens winking as it pirouetted high in the tower. The quickest way over to the path was across the cottage lawn, but the Keepers would spot him for sure. Griffin didn't have time to bushwhack behind the house, cutting his own trail through the forest—the sun would be setting soon.

He gritted his teeth and made a run for it. His sandals slipped on the wet grass, and Griffin struggled to stay on his feet. He'd almost made it to the path when the front door was thrown open and Dr. Hibbert rushed out onto the porch.

"Griffin!" she shouted. "What are you doing?"

He tucked his chin, sprinting with everything he had. Fergus and Sykes leaped down the porch steps and tore after him.

"Griffin! Let me explain!"

Griffin ran, his raincoat crackling as his elbows pumped at his sides. *I'm coming, Dad.* Griffin's lungs wheezed and his legs burned. The sound of Fergus's and Sykes's heavy breathing and even heavier footfalls seemed as loud as a landslide after a hard rain. But Griffin knew this path like he knew the way between the mounds of books, discarded shoes, and dirty laundry in his room. He knew where the half-buried tree roots jutted out of the soil and where he could cut a hairpin turn in half by leaping up the bank between ferns. He broke through the trees, sprinted across the grass, and pushed through the workroom door, slamming it shut behind him and twisting the lock.

Fergus and Sykes banged against the door seconds

later, first with their fists, then ramming their shoulders against the sodden wood. Griffin backed away. He stripped off his raincoat and dashed for the stairs. At the first landing, he wiggled out of his jeans, tying an extra knot in the sash to cinch the stola tight. At the next landing, he ripped off his hoodie, tossed it to the ground, and raced up to the watch room.

Far below, blows rained on the workroom door. Out at sea, the sun passed behind the clouds, and the sky faded to a dusty pink. Directly in front of Griffin's eyes, the gears turned, rotating the lens in the lantern room above.

He panicked. Fergus and Sykes were going to bust through that door any second, and Griffin would still be standing there trying to figure out how to open the portal.

You know more than you think you do.

Griffin squeezed his eyes shut. *Come on. Think!*

His dad was always saying how they needed to be careful with the lighthouse, that everything—from the bricks to the windows to the gears and the lens— was old as dust. You had to watch where you stepped and be careful what you touched.

The huge brass gears turned, the familiar whine sounding as the heavy lens swiveled. When his dad had been sucked through the portal, those gears had been quiet and the lens eerily still. How was Griffin supposed to stop something that big—something that was built to constantly turn, no matter what? Again, his dad's voice filled his head. *We have to be gentle with the old gears.* How many times had he said that? *Something as simple as a doorstop would send the whole thing grinding to a halt.*

Griffin felt a prickle at the back of his neck, and he turned to look over his shoulder. There, on the windowsill, perched an oddly shaped block of wood. A film of dust coated the sill around it—funny, Griffin had never wondered why it was always right there, in that spot. Every time he washed the watch room windows and wiped the sill clean, he'd picked it up and then set it back right where it belonged.

The prickles inched down his arms. Griffin picked up the block of wood and turned it over in his hands. He stepped toward the gears, and, as if he had done that very thing a thousand times before, he slid the wood into the space between spurs.

The gears stuck with a loud screech, and the lens quavered, halting mid-turn. Griffin ran up the last flight of stairs to the lantern room. He didn't know if there was something else he was supposed to do to make the portal open. But in that place where Griffin and his father had worked side by side all those years, the need to be together again shoved all the doubts from his mind.

The sun broke through the clouds just as it touched the water. All around—the bricks in the tower, the wrought-iron spiral staircases, even the floor-to-ceiling window panes that looked out on the moody Pacific—everything began to shake. The glass in front of Griffin seemed to soften and throb. Ever so slowly it began to swirl. A hum traveled up through the floor, clattering his teeth together and rattling the length of his spine.

Griffin stepped toward the bull's-eye. He lifted a trembling hand and stuck it into the center of the swirling glass. There was a sucking sound and a flash, and then all the light in the whole world blinked out.

AH, SO YOU DO WANT TO HEAR ABOUT MORE OF THE *seven worlds tethered to our own?*

I thought you might. Close your eyes, then, and listen well.

This time, picture the biggest jungle you've ever seen, with overgrown bushes, trails of tickling moss, and Tarzan vines swinging from giant trees.

Does the jungle stretch above your head? And under your feet? And as far as you can see? That's a start. See that house over there with the curving beams and sturdy pillars driving deep into the ground? That house is alive, you know. See how the leaves along the roofline all lie flat, overlapping like scales on the belly of a fish? Every building on the green world is alive.

You see, among the people of Vinea, certain branches of the family tree hum with magic. Everybody has a little of the green stuff in them. If you were to hold your forearm up against that of a kid from Vinea, you'd notice one difference. The blood that runs through her veins is green. Imagine!

A young greenwitch looks no different from the rest— her blood is pale as a pea shoot. But the more she practices, the more she comes into her strength, the brighter, and bolder the green becomes. You can spot the most powerful greenwitches from far away.

Melanie Crowder

How?

Griffin, they glow.

Some of the greenwitches practiced healing. Others tended the plants that in turn tended them. Still more created things: living sculptures and buildings and bridges leaping over vast swaths of untouched greenery.

It's not so far-fetched, not really. The greenwitches simply learned to listen to the call of the blood in their veins. They reached out to the beings who shared their world, and they asked for help. And the two developed a bond that goes so much deeper than symbiosis. Trust. That's what they cultivated, human and plant.

The magic of the greenwitches is simple: Listen. Ask. And finally, trust.

A YELLOW SKY

GRIFFIN'S FEET LANDED on solid ground, and his whole body wobbled like a toy on a shelf. He opened his eyes. He was in the lighthouse (the lantern room, to be exact) face-to-face with the swirling bull's-eye that slowed in a viscous yawn before settling back to hard, impenetrable glass.

But it wasn't *his* lighthouse. He knew that just as he knew the sour smell of a minus tide or the feeling of his father's hand resting warm and steady on his shoulder. The windows, the lens, the metal floor, and the domed roof—none of that had changed. The air was different, though. It tasted like the spark of metal after a lightning strike. The collar of Griffin's shirt was damp from soaking up the leftover raindrops dripping out of his hair. But within seconds, all of the moisture had dried in the brittle air.

He turned toward the windows, pressing his hands against the warm panes and peering up at the sky. Where was the sun? He walked in a tight circle around the lens, taking in the panoramic view. The sky was as bright as it had been at home, but the light here was yellow and diffuse, as if it had no single source in the sky.

And there was one more big difference. Whatever this tower was used for in this new world, it wasn't a lighthouse. Griffin double-checked behind him. The stairs leading down to the watch room were at his back, and the door to the gallery was on his left. He reached out a hand to steady himself. It should have been right there, in front of him.

The ocean was gone.

It felt like putting your shoes on the wrong feet or pulling your favorite sweater on inside out. Just wrong. The forest was missing too. As far as Griffin could see, the ground was a dull brown. Flat and desolate, without a tree or bush or clump of grass anywhere.

"*Somni.*" He tested the word on his lips. He knew this place. Not from a memory or an old photo. It lived in his mind with his mother's stories.

A sudden stirring in the lens at his back startled

Griffin out of his daze. The glass sagged at the center and began to swirl, the portal opening for a second time that evening. Was that the Keepers coming after him?

Griffin scrambled down the steps to the watch room and raced down the spiraling stairs. When he reached the base of the tower, a horn sounded from somewhere outside. He rushed through the door where the workroom should have been, only to stop short, stunned. A massive nave with a ribbed arch down the spine stretched in front of him. Griffin's rapid breaths echoed in the cavernous temple. He scooted to the side and clung to the wall—at least that way if someone came in, he could hide in one of the alcoves. He slid along the wall, eyes darting around the room and his hands grasping for purchase on the rough stone.

His fingers slid onto something warm and fleshy. Griffin yelped and glanced over his shoulder. Directly behind him, tucked into an alcove, was a living, breathing person. Straps held her upright at the shoulders, waist, and thighs, and her feet dangled in the air like a puppet hanging from its strings. A clear mask covered her mouth and nose, and every few seconds it clouded with moisture from her breath. The mask led to a series of tubes that disappeared into a hole in the wall behind her. Above the alcove, a single word had been chiseled into the stone.

EARTH.

Griffin screamed, stumbling backward into a pew, the sound ringing like a bell through the empty nave. He jerked like a wind-up toy, his eyes roving around the dozens of alcoves. Was his dad there—hanging limp and helpless, hooked up to those awful tubes? Griffin dashed around the nave, peering into each pained face. When he'd circled back to where he'd started, Griffin leaned against the cold stone as relief rattled through him. He sank onto one of the pews. His dad wasn't one of them.

Except for the eight alcoves with STELLA chiseled above, each one was filled with a person—somebody's mom or dad. Griffin couldn't just leave those people here, could he? He should do something. At the very least he could unhook them, and maybe they would be able to find their own way home.

The alcove closest to Griffin held a man with a thin white beard. The stone above his head read MARIS. The man's shoulders and rib cage were enormous, but his limbs hung limp, the muscles atrophied from disuse. Griffin gulped. He stepped up into the alcove, hugging the wall so the man's arms didn't brush against him. Griffin rose onto his tiptoes and reached a shaking hand up to where the mask settled over the man's nose and mouth.

Footsteps rattled down the tower stairs. Griffin jerked his hand back. He had to get out of there. He jumped down and sprinted for the door. He pushed into the yellow evening air and clattered down the temple steps just as thousands of people in the adjacent amphitheater rose to their feet. Griffin dropped to the ground and crawled behind a low wall dividing the temple entrance from the sprawling brick floor of the amphitheater, cursing himself for dashing out into the open like that. Anyone could have seen him. Slowly, carefully, Griffin peeked over the top of the wall. But no one even noticed him.

Everyone in the crowd stood perfectly still, facing the stage where a hundred men in red robes with purple sashes around their waists stared back. Their hands were clasped beneath their chins. One of the men stood a step in front of the rest, his arms outstretched. He spoke in a soothing voice, and the crowd seemed to sway, almost imperceptibly, to the cadence of his speech. Unease crept over Griffin's skin like a ruptured nest of spiders.

Those people in the crowd weren't just listening closely. They hadn't moved, not one of them, not even an inch. It was like they couldn't. Whatever that man was saying—whatever the others were up to with their closed fists and implacable stares—it was doing something to all those people in the crowd.

Griffin slunk down behind the wall again. He glanced back toward the temple doors. He couldn't move, not when everyone else was standing perfectly still, and definitely not with those soldiers in black stolas stationed at intervals along the perimeter of the amphitheater. He was trapped. And Fergus and Sykes might bust through the temple doors any second.

Just then, the priests opened their fists. The crowd seemed to shake themselves and, in perfect synchrony, turned away from the stage. They funneled out of the amphitheater, their shoulders hunched and their heads down, flinching away from the priests who watched their retreat with hooded eyes.

After the eerie silence, the sudden rush of footsteps was as loud as rainwater flooding a dry canyon. The crowd was dressed in blue stolas just like Griffin, with simple sandals on their feet. Their skin was pale and waxy, and they were tall, even the children, their limbs slender almost to the point of frailty. Each adult held a stoppered jug clutched to his or her chest.

Griffin rose to his feet. Maybe they wouldn't notice

anything different about him. His skin was pretty pale—they didn't get much sun on the Oregon coast, either. And he was tall enough, for his age. He kept his eyes on the ground as he veered into the crowd and let it carry him steadily away from the temple.

Griffin couldn't get away from those priests fast enough. He'd seen that crowd entranced—what was the term the Keepers had used? Mind control. Those priests back there had ensnared all those people, made them prisoners inside their own heads. No matter how many stories his mom had told him before bed, how many coded warnings she'd tried to give him, Griffin never would have believed it if he hadn't seen it with his own eyes.

The day was warm, but he couldn't stop shivering.

SOLDIERS, SOLDIERS, EVERYWHERE

WITH EVERY STEP Griffin took away from the temple, his panic ebbed a little. He risked a glance over one shoulder. No one was watching. No one followed him. He peered over the other shoulder, and there, at the elegant temple entrance, three figures emerged. Their stolas looked the same as everyone else's, and their features weren't so different that they stood out from the people of Somni. But Fergus was quite a bit more muscled than everyone except the soldiers, and though Sykes's height was about right, the scowl that never left his face wasn't. And even from such a distance, Dr. Hibbert's eyes seemed to bore into Griffin.

He ducked his head and hurried forward. The families to either side were talking about how they would share the daily provisions in the jug they carried, and the boy on the right and the girl on the left were in serious negotiations with their parents about how late they could stay outside and play that evening. But then the crowd in front of Griffin began to part, like a wave breaking on a jetty. All joking stopped. Parents tucked their children between them, and the crowd marched forward in steady rows.

Griffin couldn't see over the adults in front of him. He rose onto his tiptoes and craned his neck, trying to get a better look at what had everyone so unnerved. He glanced at the yellow sky above, his eyes skittering from one edge of the horizon to the other. When his gaze dropped back to the path, a large man in a black stola stood directly in front of him, letting the crowd part around him. The soldier's feet were planted wide, his muscled arms crossed over his chest. Instead of a sash at the waist, he wore a broad belt with half a dozen weapons jammed into the loops and clips.

Griffin darted to the side, falling in behind the boy and his parents. He dropped his head and watched the bricks pass beneath his feet. Sweat dripped down his forehead and ran into his eyes. He wasn't imagining things—it wasn't just his own panic that made the air suddenly seem harder to draw in. A palpable fear filled the gaps between every body in that moving sea of people.

When you're swimming in turbulent water, silt, debris, and bubbles of air churn in the water beneath you until you can't even see your own feet. Anything could be down there. A tiger shark could be inches below your toes, and you'd never know it.

Even after Griffin had moved far beyond the soldier, that feeling of being prey hung all around him. Griffin shuddered, and he looked up into the faces of the adults beside him. *They* were afraid of the soldiers.

He wasn't sure if that made him feel better or much, much worse.

Griffin wove to the edge of the crowd and darted behind a brick wall. He climbed to the top and lay flat so he wouldn't be seen. In the distance, he watched as Fergus and Sykes blended into the crowd, their eyes roving back and forth, no doubt looking for him. Dr. Hibbert didn't follow after them, though. She strode past the amphitheater, directly toward the main entrance of the rectory.

Griffin scanned the city, trying to get his bearings before he got lost in the maze of smaller roads peeling away from the main one. The tower—what he couldn't stop thinking of as his lighthouse—stood high above everything else. The temple branched off below, with the amphitheater wedged between it, the rectory opposite, and the barracks behind it. Eight main paths divided the houses as the neighborhoods (separated again into clusters of eight homes) spread out from the temple. The walls were brick, the benches were stone, and the homes were a combination of the two.

Griffin dropped off the wall and doubled back toward the temple, looking for a place to wait out the night. There was no sun to set and no moon to rise, but the sky darkened, bit by bit, and the crowds thinned as people returned to their homes. Griffin peered into each cluster of houses that curved away from the main path. There were no yards or driveways, but in the middle of all that mud and brick, a thatch of green (the only plants he'd seen) thrived in the center of each neighborhood. Beside the path and between the houses, a series of dry rivers channeled rainwater toward each garden.

Griffin turned into a neighborhood where all the lights in all the houses were out, the windows shuttered, and the doors closed for the night. He crept toward the garden and waded between hip-high plants. Around the edges, mud sculptures rose from the soil, waiting for the rains that would send them back to the ground again.

Melanie Crowder

His feet ached from all the running, and his stomach growled. He dusted off a handful of strangely colored berries and uprooted broad leaves that almost looked like lettuce. He paused, the berries halfway to his mouth. They could be poisonous. He might end up sick or worse, unable to help his dad at all.

Griffin rolled the berries in his palm. He could breathe the Somni air. Gravity pinned him to the ground, just like on Earth. So he could probably eat the food, too. He'd need to keep his energy up if he was going to find his dad. Griffin shoved the berries into his mouth, crunching on the unfamiliar seeds and letting the juice trickle down his throat. He ate as much as his stomach would hold, and then he lay back in the dirt. There were no stars in the sky, only a silver edge to the thin layer of atmosphere.

In the distance, the tower rose, a dark shadow against the clouds. As Griffin watched, the light in the lantern room switched on. The lens spun, sending its eight beams roving over the segmented city like searchlights. But then the lens slowed to a stop, and bulky shadows stepped in front of the beam. Soldiers. One by one they winked out, until only a single shadow was left alone in the tower. Where had they gone? Were there more worlds out there—more than Griffin's mom had even known about? And was

Somni taking over all of them? Sending their soldiers and their fear and destroying families just like his? The lens resumed its spinning, illuminating the silhouette of a robed Somni priest stepping into the darkness below, his dreadful work complete.

How many nights had Griffin drifted off to sleep with that same tower silhouetted against a different sky? Much as it looked the same, though, that wasn't his lighthouse. A wave of homesickness broke over Griffin, and he turned away from it all. His stomach ached and his head pounded. He curled into a ball, and his eyelids sagged closed.

"I'm coming, Dad," Griffin whispered. "Hold on a little longer. I'm coming."

Cuddle up, sweet boy. Do you need another blanket?

Remember that time we visited the aquarium, you and your dad and me? We stopped for chowder on the way there and saltwater taffy on the trip home?

Ha! I thought you'd remember that part. . . .

Think back to the aquarium. Can you picture that huge room with the bones of a gray whale suspended from the ceiling? And if you pressed your ear to one of the cones set into the wall, you'd hear a recording of a whale singing in the deep. Ah—so you do remember!

What would you think if I said there is a world out there where the oceans themselves sing to the creatures swimming beneath? And what if I told you there's nothing else on that entire world—just one unending sea, waves unbroken by land or wind or contrary currents?

Not many humans live on that world. It's not meant for us, not really. It's meant for the swimming things below. The people who live in the floating cities of Maris have developed lungs twice as large as we have on Earth. They have thick, lustrous brown skin that drinks in the sunlight glancing off the waves, and a layer of blubber beneath. But those aren't their only adaptations. As the generations passed, they learned to listen to the ocean's song. And after a time, they began to sing back.

You think I'm teasing? Try it. While your eyes soften and your mind stills, listen with everything you have. Listen for the song of the sea.

Melanie Crowder

12

THE RECTORY

GRIFFIN WOKE IN the garden, the smell of dirt in his nostrils, a feathery leaf tickling his cheek, and the last remnants of a dream playing at the edges of his mind.

A shiver rippled through him. That wasn't a dream, though. It was a memory.

Griffin raked his hand through the soil, the words of his mother's bedtime story playing over again. He looked around him, at the thin layer of low clouds, the skyline without a single tree jutting above the horizon, and the houses full of people lost in the priests' thrall.

It was true—everything she'd said, all those stories. It was all true. And suddenly the dry air that scraped past Griffin's throat didn't feel so harsh.

Maybe someday he would hear the singing oceans of Maris. But more wonderful, even, than that, his mother had been *here*. Maybe she had walked through this very neighborhood.

Longing called up the familiar ache in his chest, making his breath hitch and stutter. But it stung, too. Why hadn't she just *told* him? Why was it all hidden in riddles and stories? And why hadn't his dad taught him about the portal? Didn't they trust him?

Griffin sat up. He couldn't afford to get lost in memory and regret. His dad was still alive. Griffin had to believe that. And his dad needed him. He brushed the dirt from his stola, grabbed another fistful of greens to eat along the way, and wound back to the temple. He skirted the amphitheater and walked along the high outer wall of the rectory. The day before, when she had left the temple, Dr. Hibbert went straight there. Maybe that was where the priests were keeping his dad.

When Griffin found the servants' door set under an arch in the side, he ducked behind a low bench and watched the people come and go. Horns blasted at the top of every hour, telling the guards to rotate stations, and some of the servants, too. The guards were tall and pale skinned, like everyone else in the crowd from the night before, their hair black as ice or white as ice, with nothing in between. But the servants were smaller, with hair the colors of a sugar maple in the fall: yellow and orange and fiery red.

Griffin watched one girl about his age with a broom propped against her shoulder (and a scowl that looked permanent) waltz up to the entrance like she owned the place. He watched a woman who looked older than his grandma, her spine rounded and her head hung low, carry a bundle twice her size on her back. And then he noticed a scrawny boy with a mess of orange curls balancing a basket full of purple sashes on his head. Each time the boy stopped for a rest, setting the basket on his knee and rolling his neck, the curls bounced right back up, as if nothing had ever tried to keep them down.

Griffin jumped up and followed him. The servants' quarters weren't like the eight segmented neighborhoods where the people of Somni lived. The homes looked similar enough, but the paths in and around them wound like clutches of ivy. So instead of worrying about staying far enough back so the boy wouldn't notice him, Griffin had to hurry to keep up so the boy wouldn't round a corner out of sight.

It's a strange thing to walk through a world where the sky is yellow instead of blue. It changes everything. On Earth, the blue sky would make the dusty tan ground feel almost warm and the bleached-out bricks quaint as a Grecian sea town. But here, the yellow and the tan and the brown all blended together, and Griffin couldn't shake the feeling that he was stuck in a painting where the artist only had tints and shades of a single color to use.

Griffin licked his lips and picked up his pace. He wasn't used to heat like this. He missed the rain on his cheeks and the constant roar of the ocean. It unnerved him to be someplace so quiet; it seemed like at any moment the ground itself might rumble and groan, just to break the silence.

Finally the boy stopped at what must have been his home, dropped the basket on the windowsill, and called inside. A woman leaned out of the window, planted a kiss on his forehead, and took the basket from his hands. Griffin ducked behind the house next door and peered around the corner just in time to see the boy run across the road to where a swing and set of rings hung in the gap between roofs. He swung from the rings, his legs flapping and scraping the dirt.

Griffin darted across the road and crouched behind the wall that ran behind the boy's house. Ten minutes later, the woman placed a basket of folded and pressed sashes on the windowsill and called for him to retrieve it. The boy, pretending not to hear, dangled from the crook of his knees, his curls bouncing toward the ground and the blood rushing to his head. The woman called a second time, her tone sharper, and the boy vaulted off the swing and ran to the windowsill. But the woman was already busy inside, so she called out after him to hurry back with the next load.

The boy scurried past, no more than a step away from where Griffin hid. Pale green veins traversed his forehead, curving across his neck and spreading out over the underside of his arms and the backs of his hands. Griffin gasped, gripping the rough edges of the brick wall. He searched through his mother's stories, and it all clicked into place.

Vinea. The servants were from Vinea.

Griffin leaned back against the wall, dropping his head into his hands. Why had she bothered to tell him all those stories? Why did she need him to know about this place? Or Vinea or Maris or the rest? Was she trying to tell him about her life when clearly there was so much she had to keep from him? Did she worry he'd end up here someday? Grief ripped through Griffin's chest. Did she know that she wouldn't be here to help him when he did?

When the boy returned, he dropped the basket

and rose on his tiptoes for his kiss, just as before. But this time, when he trotted off, Griffin crept into place under the windowsill. Inside, the woman hummed while she worked. The sashes swished in the basin of water, and the iron hissed with steam as she pressed it onto the soft fabric.

Every time her footsteps approached the window, Griffin flinched, expecting to be yanked by the ear out of his hiding spot. But who would be so foolish to steal a basket of sashes from the priests? Who would even think of it?

The woman crossed to the window, set down her basket, and called to the boy. Griffin waited until he heard her exasperated *tsk* and her footfalls drift back across the room to the washbasin. Then he lifted the basket down as quietly as he could and set off at a sprint. He ran until he'd wound his way out of sight. Shouts rang out from the street behind him, first a scolding, and then the boy's high-pitched protests.

An itch between his shoulder blades insisted someone was chasing after him, but Griffin didn't look back. Sweat slicked down his temples and across his neck, sticking his stola to his spine. He panted for breath, his sandals slapping the dirt beneath him. Only when he rounded the last curve and the walls of the rectory loomed did Griffin slow to a walk.

He crossed the brick path as if he did that very thing every day. He knocked at the servants' entrance as he had seen the others do all morning. He ducked his head and hid the exposed skin on his forearms beneath the basket. The door was whisked open after the second knock, and a soldier in a black stola shoved Griffin inside. "Hurry up. The dressers have been waiting."

Griffin bobbed his head and scurried down the hall. When the soldier slammed the door and stomped back to the guardroom, Griffin let out a slow breath. He set out down the hallway, trying to reconcile what he'd seen in his mother's map with the rooms and passageways all around him. He held the basket to one side, ducking his head so he could sneak a look inside any open doorways as he passed by.

Wherever they were keeping his dad would probably be locked, with a guard posted outside. Griffin wove past libraries and offices, sleeping quarters and kitchens, and a lavish dining room with the longest table he'd ever seen. He dumped the sashes at the end of the table and nicked a polishing rag someone had left on the serving buffet. He sidled into the hall and began polishing wall sconces and the ornate window grates set into the doors, trying to look like he belonged among the army of servants. Every so often, a priest swished by in robes the color of dried blood, a pair of soldiers trailing close at his heels.

Griffin kept his body angled away and his head down, but nothing could shield him from feeling the wave of magic that swept past with them. It was like a sneeze trapped high in the bridge of your nose, like eyes boring into the back of your skull.

Griffin reached a dead end and began scrubbing the resin window set into the wall. He checked back over his shoulder, but no one was there to notice that he was completely lost.

His shoulders sagged, and a sliver of doubt worried its way in. It was getting late—and from the sounds coming from the kitchens, a big meal was going to be served soon. The last thing he wanted was to be caught out in the open while all those priests and their peppery magic filed into the dining room. Maybe he should start looking for somewhere to hide until night fell, under one of the reading tables in the library or in one of those broom closets.

Griffin doubled back, but then couldn't remember whether the library was down the hallway on the left or the one to the right. His mouth went dry. He shifted his weight to one foot and then the other. *Keep moving. Don't get caught.*

He wandered down the hallway on the right. He rounded the corner, and there, in the middle of a long corridor, was a single door with a soldier standing guard. His thumbs were looped through the belt at his waist, his fingers splayed over the dangling weapons. Griffin's throat tightened, and suddenly his legs wouldn't move him a single step farther. Was it—could his dad be behind that door?

He should be able to feel it, right? If his dad was really in there. He should *know*, somehow. A scuffle sounded behind him, and Griffin hurried past the guard and into the intersecting passageway. It was empty too. He slid to the floor in relief, his spine pressed against the wall. He gulped a quick breath and peered back around the corner.

The guard didn't look like he'd be leaving anytime soon. Maybe if Griffin threw a rock or something, the soldier would go check out the noise. Or he could start a fire and run into the hallway, begging the soldier to help. Griffin shook his head. He didn't have a rock to throw. And he didn't have anything to burn, much less a single match.

He edged forward a second time, risking another glance around the corner. Suddenly Griffin was yanked backward. A ball of cloth was jammed into his mouth and he gagged, trying to scream for help. Behind him, a door was flung open, and he was shoved backward through it.

The door slammed, and everything went pitch
black. He struggled to sit up, but something knobby
jammed into his chest and knocked him back down.
A foot pressed against his throat. Griffin closed his
eyes to shut out the dark, and a muffled wail escaped
him.

He had failed. Utterly and completely.

PART TWO

13

A PROBLEM

F I HAD SPENT every day of the last twenty-seven months as a servant in the rectory. She scrubbed dirt out of the cracks between bricks. She scoured scraps of baked-on food from the clay dishes. She carried messages from the temple to the garrison (and yes, of course she steamed open the seal to read the contents). But if she ever got to choose from the unending list of undesirable jobs, she picked cleaning the rugs. Not washing them—beating them.

Once a week the servants stretched a cord across an interior courtyard, and each of the carpets adorning the walls and the rugs padding the rectory floors was strung up and whacked repeatedly to shake the dust free. There was a special paddle suited to the task, a metal stick with a bloom of interlocking petals like an iron daisy. When her turn came, Fi slammed the paddle against the heavy carpets over and over again until she was panting and sweating and blisters bubbled up on her palms.

It was exhausting work. Maybe that's why it was her favorite. She was always too tired to think at the end of those days. Too tired, even, to miss home. That, and there was a certain satisfaction in hitting something as hard as you possibly could, as many times as you could. (Especially when what you *really* wanted to clobber was off-limits.)

None of the Vinean servants were there because they loved attending the priests. They didn't do it out of some twisted sense of devotion to the invaders who had colonized their home world. No, when the priests had taken the first batch of Vinean people to serve them on Somni, the resistance spreading its roots beneath the surface of everything their oppressors set into place had recognized an opportunity and latched on to it like a vine choking the life from its host plant.

There was only one reason Fi and the others put up with the scowls and condescension (not to mention scouring the floor around the toilets). Soon, they were going to overthrow the priests and their brainwashed soldiers, and Fi would be reunited with her family. Somni would rue the day they had even *thought* about attacking Vinea. And Fi was going to be there when they did. She may have been only eleven years old, but she had more than earned her place in the resistance. No way was she going to let whoever this kid was make those awful years of scrubbing and simpering and aching for home all for nothing.

The boy blinked, his face turning red as a poppy. She probably should make sure he could actually breathe. "Promise you won't scream if I take that out?"

He nodded. Well, as much as he could with her foot balancing on his windpipe and jamming the sash between his teeth.

"Because if you scream, I'll just shove it back in there for good, and if you can't breathe, it'll be your own fault."

The boy's eyes blinked even wider. Fi scowled to make sure he understood she wasn't somebody to mess with. And then she lifted her foot off his throat and yanked the sash out. The boy choked, sucking in deep breaths, but she didn't ease up on the paddle pinning his chest to the bricks. Gradually the shock drained from his face, and something else flushed over the tops of his cheekbones and the tips of his ears.

Fi squirmed. She knew that look. Fi and despair were old friends.

Sometimes she woke in a panic in the middle of the night, fists clutching her sheets and her body slick with sweat. She wasn't afraid of the priests catching her. She wasn't scared of the soldiers. She knew what she risked every day. But she hadn't known when she signed up how much she needed to see green, growing things all around her.

When she came to Somni, to this barren world of dry air and dry soil and a starless sky, a big chunk of her went missing. Fi had faced down the idea of dying, but she hadn't counted on living with the knowledge that she might never set foot on Vinea again. She hadn't counted on the despair.

Fi thrust her paddle harder into the boy's chest. "I saw you and the other three outside the temple last night. You thought since you snuck through the portal while the priests and their soldiers were all at their stupid ceremony that no one noticed? Think again."

The boy held out his arms, pleading. "No—I'm not with them. I swear."

Fi let up on the paddle, swinging it up over her shoulder like a scythe. She began to pace the length of the small closet. "Why should I believe you?"

The boy sputtered. "They kidnapped my dad—I just want him back."

"You mean that guy the priests brought through a couple of days ago?"

The boy sat up. "You saw him?"

"Well, from far away."

"Is he okay? How—"

"You don't ask questions," Fi interrupted, as much to keep from spilling more than she should as to keep from thinking about her own family and whether she'd ever find them while they were still alive. *If* they were still alive. "You were in the temple. You saw the dreamers hanging there—why didn't you unhook your dad and take him back to your miserable world?"

"He's not in there—I checked."

"So you decided on a whim to try the rectory? To go poking around *that* hallway and *that* door, oh, just because?"

The boy's eyes darted to the closet door. Fi leaped forward, knocked him flat again, and pressed the toe of her sandal against his windpipe. "Try it," she whispered. "That would make my decision *so* much easier."

The boy's eyes drifted closed, and he let his hands fall back to the floor in surrender. "I guessed he'd be in the rectory."

It's not that Fi didn't notice the tear slide out of the corner of his eye. She just couldn't afford to care. "How?"

"I was following Dr. Hibbert. That's where she went." His chin began to quaver, and his voice shook as he continued. "Also, my mom kind of showed me where to look."

Fi tapped a finger against her paddle. She was quickly losing patience. "And *she* is?"

The boy's eyes snapped open at her tone, and even flat on his back, completely at her mercy, defiance steadied his jaw and dried his eyes. "Her name was Katherine Fenn."

Fi lifted her foot and stepped back, bracing herself against the door. She blew out a low whistle. *Well that complicates things.* She groaned, dropping her head into the palm of her hand. If this kid's mom was Katherine Fenn, *the* Katherine Fenn, that would mean the guy the priests brought through last night was Philip Fenn? Liv and Eb definitely needed to hear this.

Fi knelt beside the boy. "All right. What's your name?"

"Why?"

Fi rolled her eyes, staring for a long moment at the ceiling. "If I'm going to risk my neck and, well, let's just say everything else that's important to me in my whole life to help you, I'd like for us to be on a first-name basis."

"Oh." He cut his eyes toward her, and his frown softened at the edges. "It's Griffin."

"And I'm Fionna. Fi for short. Hold out your arms, wrists up."

Fi ran her palm along each forearm and then leaned close, squinting at the veins barely visible below the skin. She grunted, then leaned her paddle against the door and began unwinding the sash around her waist. She picked at the seam, snapping the threads with her teeth and carefully separating the fabric. She pinched a thin sprig of malva vine between the tips of her fingers and slowly drew it out. As she had done with her own forearm the day she left Vinea for this lifeless world, she laid the vine along the path of Griffin's vein, waiting for the plant to awaken, sink into his skin, and begin the process of mingling with his blood.

His eyes bulged wide. Griffin didn't pull his arm away, but the rest of him shrank back as the vine roused, searching out his vein and shifting to line itself up with the blue shadow beneath his skin.

"Will you just sit still? I'm trying to help you here."

"What *is* that . . ." Griffin trailed off, disgust twisting his lips.

Fi didn't wait for him to pick that line of questioning back up, or to start in on others she shouldn't answer—about the resistance, or the protection the malva vine offered against the priests' mind control. It was better if she was the one interrogating him. "So after you got into the chapel and found your dad, you thought the priests and their soldiers would all just let you go free because, hey, it was really hard for you to get that far?"

The word stung as it passed Fi's lips. *Free.* In her whole life, she'd never once breathed a free breath. She'd never known a life without soldiers toppling the trees and trampling the undergrowth on Vinea.

Griffin sat up and rubbed his forearm, staring at his skin as if it didn't belong to him. He scrubbed his fingernails over the vein as if he could scratch the vine out of his bloodstream again. "I only knew I had to try to get my dad out of there before Dr. Hibbert or Fergus and Sykes got to him."

"And why is that?"

"They're going to kill him."

Fi's eyes narrowed. "So you get him out of the chapel, and away from them. Did you think the soldiers wouldn't see you two sneaking out? Did you think the priests weren't going to notice when their prisoner went missing?"

Griffin's shoulders rose and fell again in a defeated shrug. "He's all I have left. And I'm all he has too. I didn't have time to plan it all out. I just needed to get him back."

Fi crossed her arms, and then she uncrossed them. She'd spent years learning to tuck her emotions deep down, like heather seeds hiding underground, dormant for years, waiting for fire to lick everything clean. It was the first lesson Eb had taught her: Never let the priests see how you really feel. Don't give them any reason to look twice in your direction.

But the fact that Griffin was there, in the rectory, without any real plan or backup or escape route made her want to scream. He wasn't only risking his own life—Fi couldn't care less about that. Griffin was pretending to be a servant. If the priests figured out someone in their service had betrayed them, everything the resistance had planned—everything it had taken them *years* to set into motion—would be finished. And they would never get this close again.

Her family had been captured and sent to Somni

as prisoners on one of the raze crews, forced to uproot every weed or sprout growing in the wastelands. They were out there, somewhere, dying a little more each day. They were counting on her. The resistance was counting on her. And Griffin could have ruined everything, just to save his dad. That one life was worth her whole world?

Fi must not have buried her anger as deep as she'd meant to, because Griffin scrambled to his feet and grasped her arm, his eyes bright and pleading. "I may not know everything, but we've got the same enemy, right? We could help each other."

Fi wrested her arm away, lifted a finger to her lips, and pressed her ear against the door. When the footsteps had passed, she grabbed a bucket and scrub brush off the shelf and thrust them into Griffin's hands. "You do exactly what I tell you. You do not ask questions. Got it?"

"Are you going to help me?"

"That's a question."

"Well, are you?"

Fi blew out an impatient breath. "Yes. Wait—no, no, don't get excited. I wasn't finished. I'll help you *if* we get approval, and *when* the time is right."

Griffin frowned. "Approval? From whom?"

"I said no questions."

Griffin searched Fi's face for a reason to trust her, for even a trace of compassion. But the scowl was back. She wasn't budging. After a long moment, Griffin reached out and took the brush and pail. "Fine."

Fi nodded in return. "Welcome to the resistance."

14

TWO STEPS BACK

A DOOR SLAMMED deep within the rectory. Griffin jumped and hurried to catch up with Fi. The last thing he wanted to do was leave the rectory when he'd worked so hard just to get in there. But Fi was right. If he found his dad, Griffin had no idea how to get him safely home again. He couldn't do this alone, not with the Keepers and the soldiers and the priests in his way. Much as he hated to admit it, he needed help.

He should have known that rushing straight at the problem was never going to work. How many times had his dad reminded him to study a problem from every angle before jumping in? But it was one thing when the puzzle in front of him was getting the angle just right on a prism or fitting a pane of glass into its metal frame. It was another thing entirely when his dad *was* the problem, and every second he was missing felt like a lifetime too long.

Griffin plodded after Fi, the high brick walls sneering down at him with every step. Fi walked with her shoulders back and her chin high, completely at ease in the maze of hallways. She didn't look much like a servant, except for her hair, which was red as the embers of a campfire, making her pale green veins seem to leap out of her skin. Griffin held his forearm up to the light. Was that creepy vine she'd dissolved into his skin going to turn his veins green too?

When they passed one of the priests flanked by a pair of soldiers, Fi turned her face away, as if she had something more interesting to look at over there, on the brick wall. She didn't duck her head or bow and scrape. And that funny-looking stick tucked through the sash at her waist seemed more like a weapon than anything a servant would need.

Once they were alone in the next corridor over, she swung her gaze around, fixing Griffin with a probing glare. "Head down. Follow my lead." She rounded the corner and strode directly toward a half dozen guards blocking the exit. When she reached them, Fi offered her metal stick with the barest twist of regret on her lips. She made for the door, and Griffin hurried after her, his movements stiff and his steps clumsy.

"Hey, boy! Aren't you forgetting something?" Griffin stopped mid-stride, terrified. He wrapped his arms around the bucket and dropped his chin to his chest. His hair was a little too dark to pass as Vinean, and his veins were ordinary blue shadows beneath his skin. They'd spot him as a fraud the second they got a better look.

He never should have let Fi talk him away from the chapel door. He should have fought to stay close to his dad if it was all for nothing anyway—if they were going catch him no matter what.

The soldiers closed in, blocking the exit, their arms crossed in front of their chests. Each of them was tall, with a lock of pale hair combed across his forehead at precisely the same angle. And the scariest part? Their eyes were flat, vacant circles.

Before they could get too close, Fi scuttled around the soldiers and wrested the bucket and scrub brush out of Griffin's hands. "Don't mind him." She set the tools on the shelf and grabbed Griffin's elbow, yanking him out of their way. "This one's burning up with a fever. I've got to get him home in case it's catching."

The soldiers backed quickly away, arms rising to block their mouths and noses. "Well, hurry up! And don't bring him back here if he doesn't get better."

"No, no, absolutely not." Fi bobbed her head and dragged Griffin toward the exit.

As they passed under the arch, the fear fluttered out of Griffin, and he lifted a shaky hand to shade his eyes. It was all like something out of a dream—or a nightmare. He just wanted to be home, in front of the fire with his dad, drinking hot cocoa and watching the storms roll in off the ocean.

Fi banged on Griffin's shoulder to snap him out of it, and he gasped, his body remembering suddenly that he was supposed to be breathing. The air pulsed with heat, yellow and glaring. His sandals scraped on the bricks leading from the rectory to the servants' quarters. Griffin glanced to the side. Fi's face was hard, her whole body strung tight. How long had it been like this for her—soldiers around every corner, watching all the time, waiting to pounce? It was almost enough to make him forgive the bruise on his chest and the tender spot where she'd stepped on his throat. A person would need to be hard, living like this.

Griffin had completely frozen back there. The soldiers had him, and then Fi had stepped in, like it was nothing, and whisked him to safety. He had wanted to believe that he could do this all on his own. But he couldn't, that much was clear. Griffin didn't exactly trust Fi, but he was pretty sure that her kind of tough was just what he needed.

AN INTRODUCTION

AS FI VEERED off the main path to the servants' quarters, she had to shake the feeling that the guards were still watching her. That they *knew*. That they were hanging back, out of sight, and waiting for her to lead them directly to her contacts in the resistance. She made three wrong turns, just in case, then checked over her shoulder one last time before she rounded the corner and strode toward what was, for now, home.

"Almost there," she whispered.

Griffin's feet dragged along the path, his shoulders hunched in defeat. "Where's *there*?"

But Fi only faced forward, scowling.

"And when are we going back for my dad? I was

right, wasn't I? He's in that room? Behind that locked door."

Fi grabbed the skin above his elbow and pinched, hard. *"Not here."*

Griffin wrenched his arm away. "Where are you taking me? And how can I even understand what you're saying right now? Or the soldiers? We can't be all from different worlds and speaking the same language. It doesn't make any sense."

Fi sighed. Apparently the ban on questions was up. "We think it has something to do with the portal—it doesn't just move you from one world to the next. It changes you, prepares you for the world you're about to enter."

Griffin dragged his hands down his face in frustration. "And when are you going to tell me who 'we' is?"

Fi grimaced, starting up the walk of a small house with a tile roof. She pushed the front door open and turned back, tossing a look over her shoulder like a challenge. *Here's your answer,* it said. She didn't shove him through the doorway ahead of her, but she wasn't going to let him run away, either. Griffin hesitated, and when he finally stepped inside, he looked like he was half expecting to walk into a trap.

Eb and Liv immediately stopped what they were

doing. Liv drew in a hissing breath as she leaped to her feet. She had big brown eyes and thick hair framing her face like a pair of yellow leaves. She was a small woman, wiry as a juniper branch. But that was where her strength lay, in the invisibility that comes with constantly being overlooked. Beside her, Eb had gone completely still. Scary still. He was a quiet man, and he'd been kind to Fi from the beginning. Eb was an ideal spy—no one would suspect how quickly those hands could turn into weapons.

After all, he and Liv were fighters, and this was a war. They looked Griffin up and down—the baggy stola that clearly had been made for someone else, the face that, when you got a good look, wasn't Vinean and wasn't Somnite. And then they saw his shoes.

Liv raised an eyebrow in Fi's direction. Then it was back to the shoes again.

"Yeah," Fi said. "He's from Earth, and I'm not sure how yet, but he's connected to that lady you're looking for."

"For the last time," Griffin protested, "I'm not here with Dr. Hibbert. And Fergus and Sykes are chasing *me*. I'm not—"

But he was cut off by a glare from Liv. Griffin glanced between Fi and the adults. The skin between his eyebrows pinched in confusion.

Melanie Crowder

Eb circled behind Griffin, moving between him and the door. "You searched him, at least?"

Fi's eyes darted to Griffin. He was skittish enough already. "No . . . I mean, come on, he's not dangerous."

Liv strode quickly forward. "Don't be so sure. Hands out to the side."

Griffin glanced behind him. He edged toward the window, crossing his arms over his stomach. "I didn't do anything," he protested. "You have no right to—"

From behind, hands closed around Griffin's biceps. He squirmed, but Eb's grip was too strong.

"Fi," Griffin pleaded. "You said you would help me."

"Liv—come on. If you'd just listen for a sec—"

But the older woman only brushed Fi aside and began patting Griffin down, starting at the wrists and moving toward his torso. When she reached his waist, Griffin groaned in frustration. Liv undid the strap and yanked the pouch out from under his stola. She handed the loose pages to Eb and began flipping through the thin book. Her skin reddened, splotches starting at her throat and traveling up her cheeks to the tips of her ears.

"What is this?" she hissed. "Some sort of spy code?"

Griffin glared back, his mouth drawn in a hard

line. Fi groaned. The kid could be stubborn. The last thing they needed was for him to decide they were the enemy too.

Liv snapped the cover shut, shook the journal, and turned on Fi. "You think something like this isn't dangerous? What if this had ended up in the priest's hands? And you . . ." Liv squared her shoulders and closed in on Griffin.

But she never finished her threat. Though his voice was softer, Eb's words cut across everything else. "What could you possibly be doing with Katherine's drawings?"

Liv whirled around to face Eb. "What?"

"Yeah," Fi said drily. "That's what I was trying to tell you."

Griffin took advantage of the surprise on Liv's face and swiped the journal back. He stuck out his hand and Liv took the drawings from Eb, paging through them one by one before placing them in Griffin's upturned palm. She held on to one in particular—a sketch of small glass pendants—and studied the script all around the edges before adding it to the rest.

Griffin wrapped the pages reverently back around the journal and clutched the bundle to his chest. "Katherine was my mother."

Eb exchanged a long look with Liv. When he finally spoke, the tension in the room snapped, like a twig underfoot. "Fi," he said. "Start talking."

She nodded. *Took them long enough.* She set her feet wide and clasped her hands behind her back like a soldier addressing her superiors. "I spotted Griffin leaving the temple last night with the other three from Earth. And then I was making my afternoon rounds in the rectory, minding my own business and waiting for my chance to slip into the bishop's quarters, when I caught him hanging around the chapel door. I wasn't sure at first that it was the same kid—but then I saw the shoes."

Griffin peeked over the edge of his stola at his grungy Tevas.

"I knew he wasn't one of us. He's pale, though—he could almost pass for Somnite. Anyway, I guessed that whatever he was doing was going to end just as badly for us as it would for him, so I grabbed him before the priests got a good look at him." She adjusted the sash at her waist, wishing for the hundredth time that she didn't have to leave her paddle back in the rectory storeroom. "But then things got complicated."

"Because you learned who his parents are?" Liv prodded.

"Yeah. I knew you'd want to talk to him." She glanced at Griffin, her head shaking almost imperceptibly side to side. "And I think you'll even want to help him."

Liv ran a hand through a lock of yellow hair, tugging at the ends before letting it go. And then, for the first time that afternoon, her expression softened. "You did well, Fi."

Eb offered Griffin a smile. "I bet you're hungry." He crossed to a rug beneath a scattering of cushions, tossed it to the side, and lifted a grate set into the floor. The whole thing levered up to reveal a gaping hole below, and Eb climbed down a ladder that descended into the darkness. Liv reached down after him, lifted out a bowl and pitcher, and set them on the floor before extending a hand to help Eb climb back out again. They replaced the rug, rearranged the cushions, and looked up expectantly at Griffin and Fi.

"Join us?"

Fi plopped down on an orange cushion embroidered with bell blossoms. She reached out a hand to Griffin and beckoned. When he didn't budge, she said, "Look, I can't promise you anything. I don't know much about your mom or why she was so important to what we do. But I'll tell you one thing.

If you go back out there alone, you don't stand a chance. If you stay here, and if you can convince these two to help you, you might just have a shot at getting your dad out."

Liv jumped to her feet. "Philip is *here*? How?"

Without another word, Griffin crossed to the cushions. He sank into the soft pillows, over-whelmed. "Okay. So my mom traveled here, to Somni. I get that. Maybe you met her on one of her trips, or something. But it doesn't make any sense— how could you know my dad?"

"We'll explain as much as we can," Eb reassured him. "But we need to hear from you first. Start at the beginning."

Griffin dug his fists into his thighs. He didn't have to trust them. He didn't have to give them everything. Just enough that they would believe him, so they'd help him. "Two days ago, this really loud alarm went off. Dr. Hibbert and the Keepers showed up in a helicopter. They wanted Dad to do something for them. He refused, but then the alarm sounded a second time, and he said he had to help them."

"Two days." Eb drew his palm along the stubble that shadowed his cheeks and chin. "So he would still be in the chapel, maybe down in one of their oubliettes."

Liv nodded. "We have a few days before they'll move him to the temple. Griffin, I know this is hard to hear, but if the priests can't make your dad talk, they'll stick him in the temple, hooked up to a bunch of tubes, and they'll steal his dreams until there isn't any life left in him."

It had been scary enough to hear the Keepers talking about the priests and their mind control. But now that he had seen those people hanging there, lifeless—Griffin thought he might pass out.

"So they're not just going to kill him. They're going to torture him first?" The stubborn was gone, wiped clean off Griffin's face. He looked terrified, and Fi could understand why. Anyone who got in the way of something the priests wanted disappeared. Or worse. She knew that all too well. Fi bit down on her lip and turned away.

"You eat," Eb said, handing Griffin a plate loaded with an assortment of root vegetables, a dense, unleavened bread, and a half dozen dipping sauces. "We'll talk."

Fi tucked her feet beneath her and grabbed a plate. She never passed up an opportunity to eat real food. The rations handed out at the ceremony were enough to keep a person alive. But they weren't enough to keep her thinking quick on her feet or to build up any kind of muscle. Besides, there was nothing remotely satisfying about a liquid diet.

Liv leaned forward, her eyes locked on Griffin's. She was the kind of woman who, when there's bad news to tell, will speak it plain, looking a person right in the eyes. "You must know by now that the portal links eight worlds together. Each one has an exact replica of the tower in your lighthouse. But apart from that, the worlds couldn't be more different. Somni has colonized four of them; only Caligo and Stella have been able to beat back their invading forces. Our home world, Vinea, has been under Somni control for a hundred years. The priests believe our population is completely subdued, that the resistance went extinct long ago."

Eb cut in. "And we *keep* them believing this because we operate in the shadows, invisible. We're spies for now, nothing more. All the priests see when they look at us is servants. No matter how much we might want to blow up that tower or take out the priests one by one, we can't do anything that will expose the presence of the resistance here, not until we're sure we can defeat Somni for good. If the priests learn that the Vinean resistance is alive, they will slaughter every last one of us, and Vinea will be lost. Forever."

Griffin ate. And he drank in their words like someone dying of thirst.

"Your Earth is a relatively new interest. When Dr. Hibbert and the Keepers realized Somni was laying the groundwork for colonization, they searched for us. They guessed that a resistance must exist from at least one of the other seven worlds, and they believed their survival hinged on cooperation with us. They sent an anthropologist as their envoy: your mother. Katherine moved among us for years. She studied our network, and she proposed a way for our worlds to work together. She even reached out to Caligo, but their spiritual leader, the Levitator, wouldn't support any plan that might lead to more violence."

Eb paused, and Liv continued. "But after a time it became clear that not everyone from Earth shared Katherine's intentions. We began to suspect Dr. Hibbert was working against us."

Griffin picked at the bread on his plate, his appetite gone.

Liv's face clouded over, and she tensed up the way she did when something big was about to happen. Suddenly Fi wanted to reach out and cover Griffin's ears, shield him from whatever Liv had to say next. It wasn't easy, the things you had to get used to living this kind of life. Fi had never known any different.

But Griffin had, and it seemed cruel to drag him into this.

"Katherine had always known how dangerous her work was, especially those moments when she accessed the portal. If she was ever seen coming or going from this world, she couldn't turn to us for help without betraying the resistance. If she fled home to Earth, the priests would only have followed her there, straight to you, and your father."

Griffin blanched. The plate began to rattle in his hands, and Fi lifted it away, setting it on the floor in front of his crossed shins. She hadn't planned on getting drawn into all this. She was going to turn Griffin over to Liv and Eb and let them take care of it—whatever that meant. She was here to do a job, not to collect strays, and definitely not to start feeling bad for them.

Liv didn't wait for Griffin to calm himself. "Three years ago Katherine left us to return home. We created a diversion, and she snuck into the tower to activate the portal. But the priests were there, waiting for her. They knew exactly when to expect her. We were too far away to help—all we could do was watch as the beams flicked on, illuminating her silhouette high in the lantern room. The soldiers closed in and knocked her to the floor. We could only watch as their batons rose and fell over and over again."

Liv didn't wave her emotions around like a flag where anyone could see them. But replaying that moment was too much, even for her. She bowed her head, pinching the bridge of her nose and blinking in stuttering bursts.

Eb laid his hand on Griffin's shoulder. "We never saw Katherine again."

Griffin gripped the cushions beneath him, his chest heaving as if suddenly there wasn't enough air in the room. Everything went silent except for his ragged gasps. When he finally found his voice, it was weighed down, too heavy almost to be heard in the close space. "They told me she died in an accident."

"Philip never said any different?"

"I think he tried to, after that alarm." Griffin's breath slowed as questions nudged the grief back to the lonely corner of his mind where it stayed, most days. "We have to find my dad before it's too late."

Liv drew her lower lip through her teeth. "We would need to move quickly if we want to get to him in time. And going after him would mean the end of our time as spies."

Eb nodded. "Maybe it's time for the resistance to step out of the shadows and fight."

Fi's jaw dropped. She knew about the Fenns,

of course, but she'd never even considered that a broken alliance with Earth might be the reason the Vinean spy network was stuck in a holding pattern, always gathering information but never using what they learned to attack.

And that story Liv told? Fi had never heard any of it.

She looked at Griffin with new respect, shaking her head slowly. She'd thought he was going to ruin everything, stumbling around in the rectory, just begging to get caught. But maybe his sudden arrival was the push the resistance needed to finally act. Fi didn't care what got things moving. Whatever it took, she was ready. She'd *been* ready for twenty-seven months.

For this? She'd been waiting her whole life.

16

THE HUNDRED-YEAR WAR

I REACHED OUT to my contact," Liv said the minute she crossed back over the threshold, closing the door behind her and leaning her weight against it.

Griffin scrambled to his feet. "Who is it? Are you sure you can trust him?"

"You'll see, soon enough. Eb, Fi, it's time to alert the resistance. You know what to do."

Eb nodded, his hand resting protectively on Fi's shoulder as the two of them slipped out the door, joining the rest of the servants on the path leading to the amphitheater.

Griffin crossed to the window and watched the steady stream of people flow by. The day's heat had baked into the bricks, and now that the light outdoors was fading, the warmth seeped into the room. Griffin laid his cheek against the wall. "Where is everybody going?"

Liv pulled stiff curtains over the resin windows. "To the ceremony." The weight of the decision she'd just made clung to her in shadows beneath the hard lines of brow, cheekbone, and jaw.

"What ceremony?"

"Hmmm?"

Griffin could feel the heat rising into his cheeks. He'd always hated the way his face flushed so easily, announcing his feelings to anyone watching. He turned back to the bricks so Liv couldn't see the blotches of red spotting his cheekbones. "How am I supposed to do anything without giving myself away? I don't have any idea what ceremony you're talking about. And I don't get how Earth is any different from the rest of the worlds Somni colonized. Or why you have green veins—"

Liv threw back her head and laughed. The green lines angling across her neck seemed to pulse with the rhythm of her laughter. Griffin turned back to face her, sheepish. *"Sorry."*

But she only waved him off. "Griffin, this is a war we're fighting. A hundred-year war. You don't need to apologize for asking questions. And anyway, Vineans are proud to carry the heart of our green world within us, even here, in this lifeless world. It's the one thing the priests can't take away from us, at least not while we're alive."

"Okay. So the ceremony is . . . ?"

"How the priests keep everyone under their control. The citizens collect their food rations for the following day while the priests prattle on about how the temple and the stolen dreamers are the Somnites' divine right. What's really happening, though, is that the priests keep the heartstones of the sjel trees they drained set like jewels into rings on their fingers. When they hold their palms against the heartstones, the heat from their skin releases the oils inside. The priests breathe in the trees' stolen magic, and it gives them power over others' minds. Each priest is assigned a segment of the population, and as long as he lives, the people he magicks are trapped under his control."

Griffin closed his eyes, and it was right there—the dream world the way he had imagined it the first time his mom had told him the story of the benevolent trees and their dreamers. Griffin liked *that* Somni so much better than this one, and it made him wonder about all those people at the ceremony—what it must be like for them to have lost so much, to be left with only this barren world without even the freedom of their own thoughts in their heads.

"Every single person on Somni has to attend the ceremony—all the priests, soldiers, citizens, and servants. It takes all of the priests to magick the population, and they are so afraid of losing control that they don't allow anyone to miss even one night." Liv leaned close to the coarse bricks so she wouldn't be seen from outside, and she peered at the yellow skyline.

Griffin frowned. "But you're not there. Won't they notice you're missing?"

Liv chewed on the corner of her lip, considering her next words carefully. "It's what the resistance does best—move and shift beneath their notice. The priests think they have us catalogued in tidy lists, but over the years, we've slipped people in, one at a time, until our numbers are double what they think. Of course, the priests don't suspect because they think their magic makes us powerless to resist them."

Liv turned away from the window. She twisted her hands in front of her. "We have to be careful who we trust. We've been betrayed before. Think about it, Griffin. Three years ago, Somni was laying the groundwork for a massive attack on Earth. Your people had no defense against the priests' mind control. Your world could have been an easy conquest. There is no reason why Somni would stop short. But they did. Right after the priests caught your mother. Why would they do that, unless Dr. Hibbert offered them something so tempting it was worth scrapping their plans to colonize Earth?"

Griffin ran a finger along the vein the malva vine had dissolved into, thinking.

Liv pushed off the wall and came to stand beside him. She reached out and gripped his hand. "I'm sure some would call Dr. Hibbert a hero, saving her entire world from attack. But at what cost? We think she made a deal with the priests, and part of that deal was betraying Katherine."

Anger seared through Griffin.

"Your mother put herself in danger over and over again to help us. We owe it to her to keep you safe, and to help Philip, if we can."

Griffin hadn't known how badly he needed to hear just that. Relief coursed through him like flood-waters cutting away at a riverbank. He wanted to believe Liv. But he wasn't sure, not yet.

"Griffin, I need you to tell me everything you can about Dr. Hibbert. What is she doing here? Why is she back on Somni now, after being gone for years?"

His shoulders lifted and slumped again. "I heard her say they were going to kill all the dreamers to cut the tether between Somni and Earth. But that doesn't make sense. If that's all they wanted, Dr. Hibbert could have killed them right there in the temple, jumped back through the portal, and been done with Somni forever."

"Except that you're here. And Philip," Liv explained. "To cut the tether between worlds, every single person from that world has to either go back through the portal or be killed. Maybe that's why Dr. Hibbert sent Fergus and Sykes after you."

It was one thing to fit together all the pieces himself, and another to hear the thing he was most afraid of spoken out loud, plain and simple.

Griffin swallowed. "That's why she went straight for the rectory? To kill my father?" He sat up a little straighter, bracing himself for her answer.

"Possibly. But that can't be all it is." Liv began pacing the round room, her hands clasped behind her back. "There has to be more. Somni wouldn't give up on a potential colony for one person. And until we know what Dr. Hibbert offered the priests, we're in the dark."

It was quiet, with Eb and Fi gone and the neighborhood empty. Yet even the silence seemed to tug at Griffin, waiting for him to somehow find the answer everyone seemed to be so sure he had.

"That alarm meant Somni was getting ready to

come back to Earth, didn't it? And that's why Dad went to help the Keepers, because he was afraid Somni was going to invade?"

"I'm afraid so."

It made everything both better and worse, knowing his dad hadn't planned to leave—that he wouldn't have risked getting so close to an open portal for anything less than to save the whole world.

Liv handed Griffin a blanket and placed a fresh stola and a new pair of sandals beside the bed. "It's been a long day, and it's going to be an even longer night. Get some sleep."

ANOTHER STORY? CLIMB UNDER THE COVERS, THEN, AND let me think.

Remember that morning when we all woke up before the sun, pulled on our galoshes, and threw a bucket and those skinny little shovels in the back of the pickup? We drove down to the bay and walked out on the flats, the mud sucking at our feet and the gulls circling above, begging us to share our catch? Remember? It smelled like three-day-old fish out there.

I knew you'd remember the smell. That's right—it was the one and only time we ever went clamming.

Can you picture that mist? How it hovered an inch above the mud and smothered the water so you couldn't see it at all—you could only hear it slurping in and out of all the little critters' hidey holes?

Now I want you to imagine a world exactly like that— only there's no mud. No rocks or dirt, and no rivers or oceans—no ground of any kind. Just mist.

Close your eyes. Can you see the mist? There's a city floating in the distance.

Funny little skim boats drift between buildings. Birds as big as dragons and as tiny as bees fly all around; they disappear behind one curtain of mist and pop out from another like blinking fireflies.

Can you feel the mist pooling around your ankles and lifting you up? Are you there right now in your mind— standing on a pillow of soggy air? If you're feeling brave (you are, aren't you, Griffin?) take a walk on the mist with me.

No? Not yet?

It's okay. It can be hard for a person who has always felt solid ground beneath his feet to step out onto nothing, because if you walk on mist, surely you'll fall through. Won't you?

Not on Caligo.

So what keeps you from falling? Ah. The question is not what, my love, but who.

Look beyond the city, to the aerie high above. The Levitator and his fleet are there, sitting in their nest and casting their magic out, before and below them. They hold up every living thing in their whole world, from humans like you and me, to the buildings that poke out of the mist like floating islands. Bugs and birds, of course, can hold themselves aloft for a time, but even the flying lizards whose wings stretch from the curve of the rising moon to the ball of the setting sun must rest sometimes.

It's a beautiful thing to watch the Levitator and his fleet—men and women, and children in training, too— working together to hold up their whole world.

Melanie Crowder

Close your eyes—can't you see them? Almost?

Are you ready now? Take a breath, sweet Griffin, and let go.

17

THE CEREMONY

E B AND FI lined up in the sprawling amphitheater with all the servants and citizens of Somni, just as they did every evening. The crowd was separated into portions of eight, and everyone, from the elderly to the very young and every age in between, faced precisely in the same direction. The soldiers stood in a human wall around the amphitheater while a hundred priests worked their magic from the stage above.

Fi squinted her eyes and scrunched up her nose. The magic tickled—way at the back, like a big sneeze was coming. Only it never did.

She stood, straight but quivery, acting like the priests' mind control worked on her. All the servants had to pretend. They had to if they were going to guard the secret that a handful of greenwitches had survived the invasion and were passing malva vine to the resistance. So, much as it galled Fi to stand in formation, mimicking the brainwashed, listless citizens of Somni, she did her part like a good spy.

Besides, she had a message to deliver.

It wasn't that the resistance wanted to use children to do their work. But Vinea had been under siege for so long that the rule of war, brutal as it was, came to feel almost ordinary. Somni took people of all ages into their service, and the resistance couldn't afford to overlook a potential recruit, no matter how young.

Vinea had fallen in the time of Fi's great-great-great aunts and uncles. One terrible night, soldiers had marched out of the tower in droves, cutting down anything and anyone standing in their way. Vinea had had no defense—the greenwitches had never considered using their magic for violence. It had seemed too cruel, sacrificing the green so that humans could live.

The strongest among them had done what she could. She'd grabbed on to the tree nearest her, one with a taproot that dove deep, deep into the soil. With everything she had, she reached through the ground across the whole world, root system to root system.

She wrapped her whole being around the tree's trunk and asked for a warning to be sent to her people. And the trees obliged. They turned their leaves in unison to block out the moon in a blinking alarm signal that stretched around the globe.

The soldiers had pressed until they reached the edges of habitable land, and there they stopped. What had been a vibrant city of living architecture became an impassable fort built from the bones of felled trees. Prisoners were massed and shackled, awaiting transport to Somni. Vineans who hadn't been captured escaped into the wildlands, where the trees and vines and even the ground cover did what it could to hide the refugees. There, after wounds were tended to and the grieving season allowed for, the resistance was born.

If you yank a growing thing out of the ground, if you pull it up, roots and all, you can be reasonably sure it won't come back. But if the root is snapped just below the surface, only some plants will wither and die. Others will toughen, sinking their roots deeper into the ground. And the next time the tender green shoots taste the air? They won't be nearly so easy to uproot.

After the invasion, Fi's ancestors lived in a cave hollowed out of a softstone cliff. Her great-great-

great-aunt, a powerful greenwitch, had called up a curtain of creeping willow to disguise the cave's entrance. And after her death, Fi's great-aunt Una, equally powerful, had nurtured the willow until it was nearly impenetrable. The family was safe and might have been forever if they'd only ever ventured out for food and water and a little sunlight.

But that would have meant surrendering their beautiful green world to the invaders. After all, it wasn't just the people of Vinea they fought for. It was the plants, too. And the green magic. In the end, it was their devotion to the resistance that made Fi's family vulnerable.

She was four when the soldiers came.

The willow shrieked, burning in a wall of flame. Smoke filled Fi's nostrils, and screams rang in her ears. Soldiers waited at the entrance for anyone who tried to escape. Fi's aunt Ada scooped the little girl up and carried her to the back of the cave. She pushed Fi ahead of her into the escape tunnel, and they crawled on their bellies for what seemed like days. The last thing Fi's great-aunt Una ever did was to call up the ground cover to conceal the tunnel entrance.

When they emerged again into the sunlight, Fi's face was black as a bog. The only place her skin showed through was in the cracks her tears had carved into the mud. A dozen people had lived in that cave—Fi's whole family.

Two escaped.

Fi took her aunt's hand in hers, and together they dove even deeper into the wildlands. The next five years were lonely ones, for both of them. But they had each other and the green all around them.

Then, on Fi's ninth birthday, Aunt Ada asked how Fi wanted to honor their family's memory—to live in defiance of those who wished them dead or to fight back, but risk dying. Both options took bravery and resilience, she said.

Fi was surprised it was even a question.

She was a logical girl. She knew the rest of her family was probably dead. But Fi wouldn't have left Aunt Ada behind and traveled all the way to Somni if she'd really believed it. And she wouldn't have spent twenty-seven months as a servant, biting her tongue and working until she collapsed into bed every night if she didn't believe she'd find them one day.

It was why she was there, in the amphitheater, pretending it didn't make her skin burn just as hot as that curtain of willow to stand meek and biddable, while the priests gloried in their conquest.

At last the heartstones were released, and the ceremony ended. Fi and Eb split up, each searching for their contacts. It's the necessary nature of a spy network—each person only knows a handful of others. Fi had never met the people Eb and Liv reported to, and she had no idea who reported to them in turn. It was safer that way.

Fi wove through the crowd, watching for a stout woman with hair the color of a mustard seed and veins so pale they were almost white. When she spotted her across the crowd, Fi altered her course until they fell into step together. She looked once into the woman's face and then back to the path in front of her feet. "The thistle opens tonight," she whispered. "Be ready for the bloom."

The woman responded in a low voice, thick with emotion. "It will be soon?" Her hands gripped the edges of her stola.

"Very soon," Fi repeated. She didn't know the reason for the delay—why the message was for a diversion tonight and to stand ready for the full-scale revolt later. Liv didn't tell her everything, only what she needed to know to do her job.

The two separated, Fi to deliver her message twice more, and the woman to seek out the first of her three contacts. Fi raised her eyes to the darkening sky, imagining her message spreading through the crowd like water seeping into a dense root ball and dispersing until every last Vinean was alerted and ready to fight. She imagined the words finding her aunts and uncles on the raze crews, the news quenching what had been too many thirsty years.

Fi wished that had been her job. She wanted so badly to look into their faces, to show them that she was here, ready to fight for them. But someone would be getting word to the raze crews. She was sure of it. And she'd have to be content with that.

18

A DISTRACTION

ON THE DAY Fi had left Aunt Ada at the resistance command post deep in the wildlands, the stern woman had taken her niece by the shoulders and told her *Everything is connected*. She'd explained that Somni and Vinea were like seeds set loose on the same gust of wind, spinning in a slow dance together. Even if Fi and her aunt were worlds apart, they would always be connected.

Each time Fi approached the house that wasn't truly her home, she repeated those words. And she breathed deep to make room for the *missing* that was always there, lodged beneath her ribs. Missing home. Missing green things growing all over the place. Missing her family. And then she would breathe it back out, open the door, and step over the threshold.

The house was dark. Fi crossed the room to where Liv and Eb huddled together near the window. "Well?" she whispered.

"I heard back from my contact," Liv said. "We need his help if we're going to pull this off."

"Can't we just sneak into the tower in the middle of the night and send everybody back to Vinea?"

"It's more complicated than that. We have to free the dreamers and help them get up the tower steps— they'll be too weak to walk. We need to alert the resistance on Vinea so they can distract the soldiers at the fort. And then we have to destroy the portal here on Somni—I don't have time to explain it all. We have to go. Now."

"All of us?"

"You and Eb will stay here. He'll transition someone new into my place."

"You can't leave me behind, Liv. I'm the one who found Griffin. He trusts me." She didn't need to whisper. He was out of it, curled up on the cushions and snoring. Even in his sleep, he looked wounded, like he was bracing for the next round of heartbreak. "Or he almost does. He'll follow you if I'm going too."

"You may be right." Liv grimaced. "Fine. Come with us, then. But you'll have to hurry. The temple division is creating a distraction in exactly nine minutes. We need to be ready. We'll only have a few minutes of cover."

It wasn't the first time Fi had gotten instructions like those. She hadn't always lived with Eb and Liv. She hadn't always been assigned to the rectory. Each time she'd moved, it had been in the dark of night, and under the cover of a "distraction."

Griffin bolted upright, looking frantically around him. Fi helped him to stand, then turned away so she didn't have to watch as sorrow settled over his shoulders like ash raining out of the sky after a forest fire. It was too easy, looking into the face of someone else's devastation, to find yourself smothered by your own.

Fi hurried to gather her things. Aunt Ada's necklace of braided moonwort stems went around her neck. The coarse seed of a sessil tree that had been spelled by Great-Aunt Una went into her bag with a spare stola. Finally, she wrapped her shoulders in a blanket Uncle Cam had woven for her from the silky strands of osier bark.

Griffin came to stand beside her, and he watched Fi linger over each item. There was longing in her eyes, and sadness deep as a dug grave. Griffin reached out with an open palm just as she was about to put a sachet of dirt into her little bag. Fi met his gaze, and the hardness snapped back into place, her defenses up again. But he wasn't judging her. He looked, instead, like he understood what he had seen, or at least he wanted to.

She dropped the sachet into his palm, and he brought it up to his nose, closing his eyes and drawing in a deep breath. Without meaning to, Fi did the same, and it took her right back to the thick of the jungle, to the smell of wet soil and damp leaves and life budding and blooming all around her.

"You miss home." It wasn't a question. "And I guess you miss your parents, too?"

Fi held out the open bag, and he slipped the packet of soil inside. "No—I mean yes, of course. It's just that we don't think of it like that. Vinean families are more like a shared root system. There are so few children. We are raised by the generation that came before us, and the one before them. We don't have parents and siblings. We have aunts and uncles, great-aunts and great-uncles if we're lucky. We all grow up together, in one big cluster. So no, I don't miss just one or two people." She swallowed and swallowed again to let the words through. "I miss them all."

Fi sniffed to bring herself back, clipped the bag to her waist, and moved to the window. The roving beam from the temple tower had been switched off, and in the houses all around, the glow of candlelight had gone out.

Suddenly, a boom sounded to the east, and a flare of orange billowed up beside the tower. Griffin yelped and jumped back. Without thinking, Fi swept an arm out and dragged him against the wall. He was breathing hard and his eyes were startled wide, but he relaxed against her arm, and when she leaned forward again to peek out the window, he did too. Flames lit up the layers of low-lying clouds, turning them a hazy tangerine that seemed to seep onto the bricks below. Outside, the sound of people running and guards shouting reverberated against the walls. In the homes beyond the servants' quarters, people huddled together, peering out of their windows.

"Now," Liv whispered. And with barely a sound, she and the children slid out the door and along the stone wall, heading in the opposite direction of the blaze. Eb lifted his arm in farewell, and then he closed the door behind them.

Liv led them past the servants' quarters and into the Somnite neighborhoods. Fi hurried close behind Liv. Just as she only knew a handful of others in the resistance, she also didn't know why they moved when they did. For all that she'd been told, and everything she'd guessed at between overheard conversations, Fi only knew so much.

For starters, she had no idea where Liv was taking them.

Darkness blended their silhouettes into the shadows as they wove through first one segment of neighborhoods then another two. On Vinea, it was a rare thing to see the whole sky, from one end of the horizon to the other. The air was crisp, and in between branches, the stars shimmered white as meadowsweet blossoms against a blue-black sky. But the night sky on Somni was only a darker yellow, a haze of cloudy green blotting out the stars.

When the flames dimmed and finally went out, Liv, Fi, and Griffin stopped at last in front of a house on the outskirts of the city. Liv walked straight up to the door and let herself in. Inside, the home looked a lot like the ones in the servants' quarters, only bigger, and more permanent, somehow.

Houses on Somni were small, single rooms punctuated by a few resin windows and a door. Rainwater was channeled from the roof to a series of cisterns that lined the walls. Eight wedges marked the floor, which was made from the same brick that paved the streets and raised the walls, only this was thinner, and burnished smooth by the feet that had crisscrossed the room over the years.

No one came to greet them. No one lay in the beds stacked along the wall. No one sat on the pile of cushions on the floor. But still, Fi couldn't shake the feeling that she was being watched. She scanned the room, looking for the source of the twitch between her shoulder blades. Beside her, Griffin was doing the same. She took a step toward him.

The only person who didn't seem alarmed by the empty room was Liv. She stepped to the center, where the eight segments met, and she turned in a slow circle, her arms raised in the air. "We're here," she announced to the empty room. And then she let her arms drop.

One moment everything was still, and the next a whole segment of the floor dropped. Griffin and Fi jumped back. The bricks groaned as they sank, dust spilling over the edges and into the dark below. And then it stopped, just as suddenly as it had begun.

Liv walked to the edge and stepped down. She looked over her shoulder at Griffin and Fi. "Are you coming?"

And then she jumped into the gap between the sunken floor and the emptiness beneath.

THE UNDERGROUND

FI SET HER shoulders back. She wasn't afraid. She crossed to the edge and leaped.

Griffin looked around the empty room. He could just leave. He didn't have to jump down into that gaping hole—he didn't have anything to prove to anybody. Sweat broke out at his hairline and trickled down his back. How was it possible that nights on Somni were even hotter than the days?

It was one thing to do whatever Fi said when she had him pinned in a dark closet. Or to believe Liv back in the servants' quarters. But anything might be waiting for him down there. It might be the help he needed to bring his dad home—or it could be a trap. Griffin shifted his weight from one foot to the other. He closed his eyes, and his mother's voice swept in like a wave at night, her words clear as the moment she'd first spoken them: *Take a breath, sweet Griffin, and let go.*

He breathed deep, and it was her voice and her words that won.

Griffin jumped.

The ground below was closer than he'd thought. Griffin landed with a jolt that slammed into his heels and rattled the base of his neck. He stumbled, his arms flailing for balance. But Fi was there. She grabbed him under the elbows and held on until he was steady. Together they blinked, trying to see through the darkness.

Liv didn't seem to notice. She stared into the dark mouth of a tunnel that stretched, black and yawning, before them. The sound of slow footsteps approaching whispered against the tunnel walls as, gradually, a figure emerged from the darkness.

"Liv. We got your message, and of course we noticed your distraction." It was too dark in the tunnel to see the face that went with the voice. But whoever it was didn't sound happy to see them. Not at all. "You weren't followed?"

Liv shook her head.

A man's face wavered into view. He eyed Fi and Griffin, and a frown flitted over his features. "You know the consequences of coming here uninvited."

"I do."

"It was foolish to bring children, then."

Beside Griffin, Fi went rigid.

Liv beckoned to the boy. "Actually, the children are the only reason I've come. Griffin, Fi, meet Arvid."

A man with hair so blond it was nearly white stepped out of the shadows. He was willowy as a sapling, his skin so pale it held a bluish tinge.

Fi stepped sharply back. "But he's Somnite!"

Arvid ticked his head to the side. "You thought Vinea was the only world to wish an end to the priests?"

Fi gaped. "But—how?"

"You'll see," Liv said, which earned her another droll look from the Somnite. "Arvid, Griffin has something to show you."

"And what's that?"

Liv shook her head. "I know all about your protections. Get us out of this tunnel and away from those charges, and we'll tell you."

Griffin looked overhead for the first time. A pair of explosives was set into the ceiling of the tunnel. *Protections.* Griffin shuddered.

"You know what you're asking?" Again, the man's eyes rested uncomfortably on the children.

"Arvid. We don't have time for this. Hypatia's back."

His eyebrows rose sharply to meet the wrinkles that traversed his forehead. "Follow me." Arvid ducked his head, leading them on a path through the tunnels that turned and twisted, branching left, then right, then doubling back again.

Aboveground, the low clouds reflected even small dots of light, so it was never really dark on Somni, not like a moonless night on Earth when both ocean and sky were black, with only the lighthouse beams to cut through the darkness. The tunnels, though— Griffin blinked and blinked, waiting for his eyes to adjust so he could see a little ways in front of him. But it never got any better.

The farther down they traveled, the colder the air became. Griffin's ears popped, adjusting to the change in pressure. He'd never find his way out of there without help. He reached in front of him, to where Fi should have been. His knuckles banged against her ribs, and she reached back, grabbing for his hand.

And then the darkness didn't seem so frightening. So slowly he almost didn't notice, the tunnels began to lighten. First, Griffin could see his feet below him, and then the rough rock of the walls to either side. Before long, it was so bright he had to blink against the widening tunnel, and then, suddenly, they weren't in a tunnel at all.

Griffin stepped into a cavern with steel pillars reinforcing an impossibly high ceiling. In front of them, a dozen Somnites hustled back and forth, conferencing in groups, bending over broad tables to work on some sort of device, and carrying messages into the spray of tunnels that branched off the main cavern.

In the center of the roof, a single bulb shone. There wasn't another light in the whole cavern—not a candle or oil lamp or scrap of glowing lichen. Just one electric bulb. And around it, jagged slabs of translucent resin amplified the light to fill the cavern.

Griffin laughed, a short burst of surprise. "Of course! The prisms bend and focus the light source, just like in a Fresnel lens."

Arvid and Liv nodded while Fi looked around for what everyone else seemed to understand but she clearly did not. "Like a what?"

"Like the lens in a lighthouse."

"A what?"

"On Earth, our tower is part of a lighthouse, and the beams of light help keep ships safe in bad weather. The lens uses a series of prisms and molded glass to make the beams so much stronger than they would be otherwise." Griffin pointed up to the cavern roof. "They're using the same method here, to light the place with just one bulb. Except that isn't glass.

"Wait—is that a kiln over there in the corner? And are those glassmaker's shears on the workbench? Why would you—"

"Griffin." Liv's voice carried a wary note as she cut in. "Show Arvid your mom's drawing, would you? The one with the necklaces?"

Griffin hesitated. He didn't know why Liv had brought him here. He didn't know who this guy was, and the last thing he wanted to do with his mom's things was wave them around for strangers to gawk at. He'd promised his dad that he wouldn't show the journal to anyone. But the drawings were different. They'd hung in plain sight for years. Maybe they were meant to be seen and shared.

Griffin drew his lower lip through his teeth. At some point, he was going to have to trust somebody. He lifted his shirt and reached into the pouch at his waist, carefully extracting the drawing Liv had asked for and holding it out for the Somnite to see.

Arvid's eyes widened as he stared at the page. "His mother's drawing? So this is Katherine and Philip's boy?"

Shock crested like a sneaker wave behind Griffin. The last thing he expected was for this Somnite to know his parents too. Every time he thought he might be beginning to understand how things worked here, something new knocked him flat.

When Liv nodded, Arvid knelt down to clasp Griffin by the shoulder. "But—what are you doing here? This is the last thing your parents would have wanted."

Liv answered, "We found him in the rectory, trying to sneak into the chapel. He was looking for his father."

"Philip is being held by the priests?"

"Please," Griffin begged. "Please help me find him."

No one spoke, and a long look passed between the adults. Arvid peered down into the boy's face and back to the drawing in his hands. When he stood, his hand fell away from Griffin's shoulder.

"I'm sorry. As much as I respect your father, I can't risk what we're building here to help you."

20

SACRED

ARVID AND LIV crossed the cavern to a second tunnel carved into the far wall and disappeared into the darkness. Griffin looked like he'd been flattened by a windblown tree, and Fi didn't have a clue what to say. There wasn't anything anyone could say to soften that kind of blow.

Fi was grateful, of course, that Arvid had decided against blasting that tunnel and burying them all inside. She was furious for Griffin—that he'd come all this way, that he'd trusted her, only to be shut down. But more than any of that? She was confused.

Fi had spent the last few years giving everything to her work in the resistance so Vinea could be liberated. She'd always known there was more to the plan than she was aware of—that's just the way it worked. Of course they wouldn't tell her all the little details. But learning that there was a whole network of Somnite rebels she'd never even heard of? What else weren't they telling her?

It's like when you're trekking through the under-brush, and you think the person in front of you, the one you've been counting on to lead the way, is holding the branches back long enough for you to pass, so they don't slap you in the face.

Only she's not. She never was.

Fi followed after Liv and Arvid, pulling Griffin along with her. The tunnel went dark as they left the cavern, and then slowly brightened, the air warming as they drew closer to a second one. The light was different this time, gauzy and dim. The air was wet, like the jungles of Vinea. Fi lifted her face and closed her eyes, a wave of homesickness wafting over her like steam. The air laid droplets of moisture on her cheeks and in her hair. The fabric of her stola clung to her calves instead of swishing and twitching with every step. When they stepped out of the tunnel at last, even Arvid, who must have seen the sight every day, stopped and stared reverently upward.

This cavern wasn't empty like the last one, echo-ing with the sound of people going about their work. This one was full. Trees stretched from a bed of dark, rich soil clear to the roof of the cavern. You could only see a little of the canopy, though. The first few branches were distinct, but the next were obscured by a layer of thick, wet clouds. On the ground, between the staggered tree trunks, beds were planted in the soil, some occupied and others empty, waiting for nightfall.

Fi rushed forward, and she fell to her knees beside the nearest one. She ran her fingers over the slender shoots twining together to form a springy weave that would soften in just the right places when a person lay down upon it. The shoots rose ever so slightly to press against her hand. When Fi turned back to the others, her cheeks were wet, and the bitter twist of her lips had been smoothed away.

"A greenwitch was here?"

"Several years ago, yes. Katherine brought her. She insisted that we had to work together, all of us, no matter what world we were born into, if we were going to defeat the priests. She hoped that united we might be able to achieve what eluded us separately."

"And the greenwitch? Is she still alive? Did the priests catch her?"

"They did. I'm sorry. She was very strong—the blood in her veins was too bright for her to blend in anywhere on this world."

Arvid turned to Griffin and gestured upward. *"This* is why Dr. Hibbert is such a threat. In the early days when Earth's Keepers made contact, Philip gave us the mechanism to create light deep underground. Dr. Hibbert nurtured the few sjel tree seeds we'd been able to save into saplings, and she planted them here. The Keepers gave us back our trees, and the few of us trusted to travel below the city learned how to dream again."

Griffin walked over to one of the trunks and leaned against it, looking up. His face was full of memory, and of loss. Fi craned her neck upward. "What do you mean, dream again?"

Arvid clasped his hands behind his back. "Our dreams leave our bodies with our breath, and they rise to create those clouds. The clouds sustain the trees who, in turn, offer communion with us. That connection makes us impervious to the priests' mind control."

How many times had Fi stood in the ceremony, loathing the brainwashed people of Somni for their weakness? She'd never once imagined what it must feel like to them—to be trapped inside their minds, held against their will. Fi shuddered, following Arvid as he led them to the cavern wall, where several pieces of paper were preserved inside a resin case.

One was a drawing of sjel trees. Tiny script detailing soil composition, ideal humidity levels, trimming, and pest control filled the margins. Another was a diagram of the prisms on the ceilings of the caverns. A third contained instructions for sustainable sap harvest. The last was a sketch of three people. One, Fi recognized as Dr. Hibbert. The other two—she hardly needed to glance at Griffin's face to know she was looking at a portrait of Philip and Katherine Fenn.

Griffin crossed to the wall and trailed his fingers along the sheet of resin covering his parents' faces. They weren't smiling in the sketch, but they didn't need to. They fit together—her tucked under his arm and him leaning instinctively toward her. Griffin pressed himself against the resin, wishing he could cross over to that time before anything had torn his family apart.

Arvid lifted the top of the case and placed the new sketch beside the others. "When we lost Katherine, Earth went silent, and we've been working blind ever since. This is what we've been missing. So thank you. For returning hope to us."

Fi leaned closer, inspecting the recent addition. There were two parts to the drawing, a sketch of a man kneeling beside a box with fire inside and inserting a long metal rod through the opening. Around it were drawings of tear-shaped pendants. Irritation chafed at Fi like a rash. "I don't understand. What does any of this have to do with toppling the priests and kicking the soldiers out of Vinea?"

Arvid turned to face her. "Here in these caverns, we've made a haven for ourselves, and we're learning to use the magic of the communion between humans and trees. But when we leave these tunnels? The dreams fade. And magic eludes us.

"You must understand that the first world the priests colonized was their own. Of course we'd like to free Vinea from Somnite control. But we also want this world back. Desperately. We want the sacred sjel trees to thrive again above the surface. We want our own dreams to feed them, not the coerced ones of prisoners. It poisons the magic of this world. It twists it into the vile stuff the priests wield, until it's something ugly we no longer recognize."

Liv turned to Fi. "Because we joined our blood with the malva vine before we ever came in contact with the priests' mind control, it doesn't affect us. So what's stopping our resistance from overthrowing Somni?"

Fi frowned. The answer was painfully obvious. "The soldiers. They're everywhere."

Melanie Crowder

"Exactly. We can spy on the priests. We can collect information. But we can't infiltrate the soldiers' ranks."

At this, Griffin spoke up. "Because all the soldiers are from Somni. And they look different from you Vineans."

Fi was about to snap back, something about stupid questions and even stupider answers. But then: "*Oh*. The Somnite rebels *could* blend in with the soldiers."

Liv nodded. "We haven't risked coming out of hiding because we always knew we couldn't do it without their help. When Katherine was betrayed, trust between our worlds eroded. We stopped working together. And all our plans to attack the priests were put on hold. But now, thanks to you and Griffin, we're talking, for the first time in years."

Fi turned on Arvid again. "Then what's stopping you? Why didn't you help us to free Vinea ages ago? And how are necklaces going to help anything?"

Arvid frowned. "The pendants join the magic of our worlds. They are made from glass fused with a small amount of the sjel trees' lifeblood, given willingly. Philip designed them, and we believe that by wearing them we can take the sjel trees' magic above-ground with us.

"You see, since we are exposed to the priests' mind control at birth, your malva vine doesn't work on us. Without the sjel trees growing wild on the surface like they did before the priests wrested control, we need a way to take their essence with us when we travel above. And we need to be able to pass that essence to the sleeping masses so that when Somni rises up, all of us rise together. Because even if we took over the military, liberated your dreamers, and evacuated every servant from the temple, we'd still be left here with a hundred priests holding our citizens under their sway. It will never end, not for us, not unless we can defeat the priests. And for that, we need those pendants, one for every single Somnite."

Fi backed up until she was pressed against the cavern wall. It all sounded so hopeless. To hear it laid out like that—everything that needed to line up perfectly in order for the resistance to win—it seemed impossible.

Liv came to stand beside her, and she draped her arm over Fi's shoulders. "If the priests are taken out, everything else will fall. But if we only try to get all the servants home again, even if we can manage that, and even if every last soldier is kicked out of Vinea, Somni will still be under the control of the priests. And they'll never stop looking for a way to come back to Vinea."

"You forgot to mention the raze crews. We have to get them out too."

Liv patted the girl's shoulder, but she didn't meet Fi's eyes.

"Liv—" Fi sputtered.

"This is a war, Fi. There are casualties."

"You can't just give up on them! They're Vinean too. They're just like us." Fi's voice thinned until it was shrill as an icy wind cutting through a stand of pines.

Liv turned on her then. "Fionna, once the priests know their servants are spies, *if* the resistance survives, we can never go back to the way things are now. We've only got one shot at this."

"But why can't we free the raze crews at the same time?"

"It's too much exposure. The crews are stretched out all over the wastelands. It would take too much time to locate them all, much less free them. And if we tip our hand just to save the raze crews, giving up the secret that the priests' mind control doesn't affect us, we'll have lost the element of surprise, and the whole effort will fail. I'm sorry, Fi. It's simply too risky."

"But—"

"Enough. They knew what they signed up for. There's nothing we can do for them now."

21

MIXING MAGICS

GRIFFIN HAD SPENT enough time with Fi to get that she wasn't all barbs and spines. It's just that she knew when to hide what she felt deep inside. She knew how to hold it there, let it smolder until it was time to let everything burn down. A few days ago, Griffin would have melted when Arvid refused to help. He would have collapsed, giving up on himself and his plan. But not anymore. Griffin took all that frustration, he took the defeat, and he tucked it away.

He needed to think.

Fi had stormed off after the argument about the raze crews. Liv and Arvid were on the other side of the main cavern studying a map of Somni. They'd probably forgotten all about him now that they'd gotten what they wanted.

So Griffin was left alone with his thoughts. He leaned against the cavern wall, and he dug under his stola for his dad's journal. He glanced over his shoulder to make sure no one was watching, then flipped to the pages on Somni. The first one was a diagram of the bull's-eye, noting the subtle differences in the glass. The next page was about atmospheric conditions and the altered melting points of various metals. The third held instructions for mixing an unfamiliar compound into the glass. Griffin hadn't thought twice about that entry until he'd seen the hungry way Arvid had stared at his mother's sketch, the way the Somnite spoke of fusing the sjel trees' lifeblood with glass.

Mixing magics from two worlds.

It was a daunting idea. And a powerful one. Griffin eyed the kiln across the cavern. It would take a few tries, but he was pretty sure he could do it. He wanted to rush over there and get started right away, but the day had already been impossibly long. He could barely keep his eyes open.

You can't rush things when you work glass. If you skip straight from the coarsest grit to the finest one, the polish is never going to be smooth enough. If you don't let the glass cool bit by bit when you take it out of the kiln, the whole thing will shatter. It was one of the first things he'd had to learn in his dad's glass studio, and it hadn't been an easy lesson.

Griffin needed to get some sleep. Once his head was clear, he could take his time, make exactly what Arvid needed. Then Griffin would have the upper hand. He wouldn't let Arvid say no. He'd force the Somnites to rescue his dad.

22

BENEATH THE TREES

A SPY IS no good on an empty stomach. So while Liv and Arvid talked strategy, Griffin and Fi were fed until their bellies were round and their eyes began to droop. They were tucked into beds beneath the sjel trees and left alone with their thoughts.

"Fi?"

"Yeah?"

"I wanted to say—I'm sorry."

Fi dragged her eyes away from the shifting cloud and turned toward Griffin's voice. He lay on his side, his head pillowed on his hands. He looked so earnest.

She sighed. "For what?"

"When I came here, I was so worried about my dad and so hung up on trying to figure out who I could trust and who I shouldn't that I didn't think about anyone else. I never thought about what this whole mess must be like for you."

"Oh." Fi interlaced her fingers under her head and raised her eyes once again to the canopy. There was no breeze in the cavern, but if you watched long enough, if you let your focus slip and your soul soften, the highest branches seemed to bend and sway, as if they were reaching out to draw the dreams up.

"I should have trusted you."

"Yeah."

"I do now, though, if it's not too late."

She didn't answer, but the beginnings of a smile pulled at her lips, tugging them up at the corners.

Griffin propped his head on his hand. "My mom told me a story about Vinea once. She said it was beautiful."

"It is." There was a long pause, and when Fi continued, her voice was barely above a whisper. "I don't know what Earth is like—I heard you have greenscapes. But it's not the same. On Vinea, the green is more than just the landscape. It is the beating heart of our world. You have to feel it, maybe, to understand."

"You miss it."

A groan slid between Fi's lips before she clamped down on it. Her voice, when she finally spoke again, was like a dead thing. "Vinea is dying, bit by bit. The priests are furious that the greenwitches kept the green magic from them. The mind control may not work on us, but we bleed like everyone else. So there are soldiers everywhere, making sure we remember how easily they can make us bleed. They steal us from our families, force us to work as servants, and then, when we're of no more use to them, they send us out of sight, to the raze crews. To die."

Fi's fingers drifted down to the shoots that formed the bedframe beneath her. The plant softened at her touch, the faint pulsing beneath its skin soothing her raw edges. "Do you have any idea what it's like for them? They grow up in a world overflowing with life, and then they're dragged here and forced to stamp out anything that even tries to grow."

But Griffin had settled on something else Fi had said. "So, after you're done being a servant, you'll be sent to the raze crews? You're never going home? Not ever?"

Fi closed her eyes as pain squeezed her lungs. "No." It was barely above a whisper. "We know when we give ourselves up to the soldiers that there's no going back, not unless we destroy them."

"Wait—you gave yourself up?" Griffin's brow creased in confusion. "Why would you do that?"

Fi sighed. "The soldiers on Vinea do sweeps of

the wildlands. They don't like to go out there—they think the jungle is against them. And they're right. But the priests demand more servants, all the time, so the soldiers burn and slash and capture anyone in their path.

"Then, in the middle of the night, the resistance sneaks into the fort and trades their own members for the innocents who were captured. They go free and we are put in their place to be sent here. We know when we leave Vinea that we'll never go back. We'll be servants, and then, when the priests are done with us, we'll be sent to the raze crews."

"But the resistance is going to fight back now, right? And then you can go home?"

Fi's eyes grew hot, and her insides twisted in on themselves. They weren't going to fight for everyone. Sure, the resistance was going to bend over backward to save the people of Somni. And Earth. And to rid Vinea of soldiers.

All that was good. But Fi hadn't signed up for the resistance to free people in other worlds she'd never even heard of. She came to Somni to find her family. To free them from the raze crews. And now—the resistance had forgotten them. She knew what it felt like to be angry. She was used to grief. But betrayal? That was new.

If you know you're going to take a punch, at least you can brace for it, clench your muscles, and tuck against the blow. It's the hits you don't see coming that knock you flat.

The cavern was humid; Fi shouldn't even need the blanket she'd pulled taut under her chin. But she was shaking, her legs trembling and her jaw chattering no matter how tight she ground her teeth together. After all those years working for the resistance, questioning nothing, it was like a part of her was sloughing off; a second skin was being shed.

Fi couldn't trust them anymore. And maybe they shouldn't trust her, either.

ALL TUCKED IN AND READY FOR YOUR STORY?

I could keep going, you know—a different one every night about a new and mysterious world. I haven't told you yet about Arida, the desert world, or Glacies, the ice world. And I could spend all night describing the wonders of Stella, the night world, and its beautiful darkness.

But there is a point to all this, of course. Stories usually have a point, don't they?

This time, sweet boy, it's magic.

I knew you'd like that!

You've heard some of it already. Somni's magic is in the mingling of sjel trees and dream clouds. And Vinea? That's right. The greenwitches—it is a wondrous thing to watch them work. Caligo's Levitator keeps everybody floating in those mists. And Maris's magic is found in the music of the seas.

What's that? You think Earth doesn't have any magic? I suppose you're right, in a way. Our world used to hold so much more. But there are glimmers left, if you know where to look.

Think, Griffin. You know the answer.

No?

In the beginning, Earth's magic was found in its elements. Carbon. Gold. Manganese. Helium. Boron.

Calcium. And yes, did you guess? Silicon. If you mix silica with lime and soda, what do you get?

Glass.

That's right! You'd spend all day in the studio with your dad if he'd let you, wouldn't you?

But here's something I bet he never told you: Glass is magic.

No, I am—I'm being perfectly serious.

If you ever wanted to visit one of those wonderful worlds, do you know what you'd need?

Yep, magic. And the kind of magic you'd need? Glass.

It's the way between worlds.

Tonight while you sleep, search your dreams, my love, and see if they don't tell you it's true.

Melanie Crowder

DREAM CLOUDS

WAKING BENEATH THE sjel trees was different from any other kind of sleeping or waking Griffin had ever known. For the first time since his father had been kidnapped, Griffin didn't feel utterly alone. It was as if his dreams had been guided by someone— or something—else.

Griffin watched the cloud weaving like gossamer between branches. Were his dreams a part of that cloud now too? He arched his back and stretched his arms over his head. He'd dreamed of his mother again, replaying one of her stories. It was as if she were right there, cradling his head and speaking in soft tones while his eyes grew heavy and his mind became still.

Missing her hadn't faded as time passed, like

everyone had said it would. If anything, here, beneath the trees in the cavern where she must have lain too, her voice seemed stronger, and her words carried even more forcefully. Overnight, clarity had settled in, bringing calm along with it.

Fi's bed was empty, the sheet twisted into a ball in the corner. Griffin wiped the sleep from his eyes and stumbled out of the dream cavern, through the darkness of the tunnel, and into the first cavern. He blinked against the light and crossed the busy room to where Liv, Arvid, and Fi were leaning over one of the broad tables.

"I know the deal Dr. Hibbert made," he announced. "And I'm here to make one of my own."

Fi's eyebrows shot up in surprise as they all turned to stare at Griffin, the map of the city and the plans they'd been making forgotten.

"What do you mean you want to make a deal?" Liv asked, her tone hard. "Do you know what we have already risked to help you?"

"And I'm grateful. But like you said, we can't rescue my dad without Somnite help, and Arvid is refusing to help us."

"Listen—"

"No. *You* listen." Griffin rubbed a hand across his forehead. "My mom used to tell me these stories. I thought they were just this silly, sentimental thing between us, until I came here. But now I get that she was telling me the things I needed to know if I ever ended up here, like this."

"Go on," Liv prodded.

"She told me about the eight worlds and the magic they held. She told me that Earth's magic was in its elements. The strength in some of them has faded, but silicon—that one's still as powerful as it ever was." Griffin looked from one face to the next, expecting them to react—to say something. "The day I came through the portal, the Keepers were packing up all these canisters of silica."

Still nothing.

"You need silica to make glass. Think about it. Somni doesn't need to colonize Earth. Not if they get our magic anyway."

Fi tore at the edge of a ragged fingernail. "What would the priests want with a bunch of glass?"

"Well, none of the other worlds have the raw materials needed to make glass," Arvid said. "The only glass on any world other than Earth is in the tower."

Griffin nodded.

Liv sucked a breath through clenched teeth. "You think they are trying to make another lens? To do what—reopen the way to Stella?"

Arvid raised his eyes to the ceiling and blew out a slow breath. "Or any world that defeats them."

Fi's eyes grew round. "So even if we win—even if we get back home and beat the soldiers and destroy the lens leading to Vinea—even then, they could just make another one and attack again any time? We'll never be free of them?"

Liv drew a hand across her mouth. She nodded soberly. "So *that* was the deal Dr. Hibbert made. She sends a steady supply of silica through the portal, and in return, the priests leave Earth alone."

The cavern fell silent. Motes of dust drifted down from the ceiling, and the amber light settled over grim faces. Griffin sucked in a breath. This was going to be the hard part.

"We all agree that we have to stop the priests. You keep saying you're not ready to attack, but it *has* to be now, before they figure out how to turn raw silica into glass."

Arvid lifted a hand to silence him, but Griffin wouldn't stop. "Do you want to guess why they pulled my dad though the portal? Not Fergus? Not Sykes? Not any of the other Keepers?"

He glanced between Liv and Arvid, his confidence building. "Because my dad is a glassmaker. He can make those bull's-eyes, easy. If the priests have enough glass, and the knowledge in my dad's head and his hands, their portals will never be closed for long. Still feel okay about letting the priests do whatever they want with him?"

"Griffin," Arvid scolded. "None of us are *okay* with any of this. But each of us has to do what's best for our own world and our own people."

"Sure—just like Dr. Hibbert did." Griffin watched his words find their target and sink their barbs in.

"Here's what I'm offering: I'm going to make you six of those pendants. You're going to pick six of your best fighters to wear them when we go rescue my dad. The lifeblood inside the glass will shield their minds from the priests. It's what you said you needed—to be able to carry the sjel trees' protection with you outside of these caverns."

"You?" Arvid asked, incredulous. "You can make those pendants?"

Griffin braced his shoulders and faced down Arvid's scorn. "My dad made me his apprentice. I can't do everything he can, but I can do this. After we rescue him, together we'll make you enough pendants for every single Somnite. Even the soldiers, if you want. You'll be free of the priests forever."

Arvid watched Griffin carefully, weighing what

he offered against everything the fragile rebellion stood to lose.

"If my mother were here, she'd be telling you that we all need to work together, right? I have every reason not to trust you, and not to help you. But it's what she believed in, enough to risk her life to make it come true. So I believe it too. I'm going to help you. And you're going to help me, too."

Melanie Crowder

24

THE CHAPEL

GRIFFIN SPENT THE morning huddled over the workbench. He moved between the fire and his tools and back again. He pulled at beads of molten glass like they were tree sap. He checked his work against the instructions in the notebook and started over again. And again.

Fi watched from a distance. Griffin had changed. Belief had straightened his spine, and confidence had lifted his chin.

She mulled over an idea of her own. It was risky. It might be all for nothing. But the night before, while she'd lain beneath the dream cloud and breathed the wet air, one thing became perfectly clear.

If she were cast aside and sent to the raze crews, that wouldn't change her—Fi would still be Fi. She'd still hate Somni with everything she had. She'd still do anything to free Vinea. So she had to believe that it was the same for the rest of the Vineans on the raze crews, that they were still fighting, even in their chains. They may not have had any way to communicate with the resistance, but they'd be ready and waiting to rise up when the time came.

She might not be able to do much, but she could let them know that the time had come. She could send them a sign.

When the third horn sounded after lunch, Fi stood in line with all the servants waiting to enter the rectory. She held her breath as she crossed beneath the arch. Sure enough, the soldiers guarding the door had been replaced with Somnite rebels in black stolas. Griffin's pendants dangled from cords around their necks. Liv walked two steps in front of Fi, and Eb was a little ways back. Beside her, Griffin was strung as tight as a trip wire. He wouldn't stop fidgeting.

"Quit it," she whispered. "Count your steps, like I told you to. Forget everything else."

Liv had been clear about the plan. There would be two phases. First, they'd infiltrate the chapel, free Philip, and, in the process, grab any last bits of intelligence they could. Whatever happened, Somni would know their servants had betrayed them. The resistance would never get a chance like this again. Next, while the Vineans stormed the tower and opened the portal to Vinea, Arvid would slip back down to the caverns with Griffin and Philip. While the priests and their soldiers were busy defending themselves against the insurrection on Vinea, the Fenns would construct enough pendants for every Somnite under the priests' control. Then, and only then, would the Somnite rebellion begin. The priests would have to defend themselves on two flanks. And the outnumbered, outgunned Vineans would stand a fighting chance.

But there was another part of the plan Fi hadn't shared with anyone. She dropped her hand to her side and felt for the stiff paper strapped against the long muscles of her thigh. If she'd had a greenwitch's powers, she could have asked the sjel trees to lend one of their broad leaves. But she didn't. So she had to be content with sneaking back to the cavern when no one was looking and swiping one of the maps off the table. It would have to do.

Fi should have been nervous. She'd never disobeyed Liv. Ever. She'd never wanted to, before this. But instead of nerves, she only felt fire beneath her skin. She followed the others through the rectory and to their posts. She grabbed her paddle from the closet and trailed after Liv into the courtyard where the first set of rugs were being strung up. She handed Griffin a bucket and scrub brush for cleaning the bricks and stepped up to the first rug.

Fi gripped the handle of her iron paddle with both hands and swung with everything she had. The metal struck the heavy weave with a satisfying *thwack*. She swung and swung until chunks of hair stuck to her sweaty cheeks and her breath hitched in her throat, until Liv laid a hand on her shoulder, calling her back to the hot courtyard as a priest strode by in his flowing red robe that swished like silk across the rough ground. Soldiers marched past—real ones, not rebels in costume. Anger stirred inside her like a swarm of stinging insects.

The fourth horn sounded. Fi ducked her head, and she counted her breaths. One hundred. Two hundred. She tucked her paddle through the sash at her waist and pulled Griffin with her into the main hallway. Two dozen others broke off toward the east wing to create a diversion. Liv ducked into a supply closet and emerged gripping a crowbar with razor-sharp tips. She led her team straight to the chapel.

This was it. If Arvid's team had done their work, the chapel door would open wide for them. But if they'd failed to replace the chapel guards, the resistance would be over before they even got a chance to fight back. Fi rounded the corner into the long corridor and headed for the locked door. She held her breath as she drew even with the soldier standing guard. And then, like she had imagined a thousand times before, the guard stood aside to let the resistance stream through. When the door swung shut behind them, the corridor filled again with servants scraping the grit from between bricks, polishing the statuary, and dusting the seam between ceiling and wall as if nothing out of the ordinary had happened.

Fi's relief only lasted as long as it took her to glance around the room. They had chapels on Vinea, but they were nothing like this. They were buildings only so much as the shape of the trellised vines arced overhead and a lush carpet of moss padded the ground. There were no walls to trap the song inside and only enough leaves to funnel away the rain; not so many that they would keep out the light. Vinean chapels were holy spaces.

This place? There was nothing sacred about it.

It wasn't even a chapel. It was an interrogation room. Bolted to the center of the floor was a metal chair with straps to hold a person down at the wrists, chest, and ankles. The tile around it was pocked by metal grates covering round holes in the floor. Oubli-ettes. Cells you could only exit and enter through the ceiling.

Fi dragged her eyes away from the holes in the floor and dropped to her hands and knees, checking behind and beneath the furniture for hidden com-partments. Everyone had a job. Some were look-outs in the interior corridors. Others rifled through the wall of cupboards, searching through the files and records, gathering intelligence. Hers wasn't a dramatic job, but it was an important one. What-ever happened after this, the element of surprise the resistance had protected for so many years would be gone. They would need all the information and all the secrets they could get their hands on.

And they had to move quickly. There may have been only one entry from the corridor into the chapel, but three hallways snaked away from the opposite wall. The resistance had taken years compiling a map of the rectory, and those hallways weren't anywhere on that map. They had no idea where they led, or who might appear out of them at any moment. Fi's hands trembled as she ran them along seams in the wall and the backs of drawers. Her fingertip snagged on a latch tucked under the base of a chest of drawers just as Griffin cried out behind her.

"Dad!" He leaned over a grate in the floor, his fingers grasping the metal and pulling with all his strength. Griffin strained, his arms shaking as he tried again to lift the heavy grate.

Arvid and Eb hurried to his side, and together they lifted the metal away. Arvid grabbed the ladder propped against the wall, lowered it into the hole, and climbed down. Muffled voices sounded below, and then the men slowly climbed out together, Philip leaning on his old friend and struggling to lift himself out of the prison.

When Philip crawled away from the opening, Griffin dropped to the floor and threw his arms around his dad. He squeezed his eyes shut and held on as tight as he could. The air seemed to spiral around them, motes of dust called up to form a curtain of quiet. They were trembling, both of them, Philip shuddering as sobs racked through him, and Griffin shaking with grateful, incredulous laughter. Or maybe Griffin was crying and his dad was laughing. Maybe both. Maybe everything all at once.

Fi watched, an ache swelling her throat. The kind of ache you feel when beside your joy for that other person, your own grief rises up to meet it.

"Griffin?" Philip pulled back, his hands cradling his son's face. "What are you doing here?" But it wasn't the kind of question that needs an answer. Griffin gripped his dad even tighter, his face drawn so sharply in relief it looked no different from pain.

Fi pried her eyes away, turning her attention back to the chest of drawers to give them some privacy. She fiddled with the latch until it clicked, the panel dropped, and a weight fell into her hands. Fi slid the false drawer out and set it onto the floor, slowly so it wouldn't clunk against the bricks below. The drawer held a ring of keys that jangled and shook as she drew them out.

Fi rolled them over in her palm, excitement shivering through her. To be hidden like that—they must be important. The raze crews were chained together. Was it possible that she'd found the keys to free them? With trembling fingers, Fi fitted the drawer back into its hiding place and turned to face the room, tucking the keys into her sash. Griffin and his father still hadn't gotten up off the floor. Philip was weak and filthy. They were never going to get him out unnoticed.

"We have to go." Fi edged toward the door. Nobody moved. "Now. Let's go," she said again, a little louder this time.

Philip lifted his head, seeming to see the rest of them for the first time. "Wait. We can't go yet. Dr. Hibbert's here."

"We know," Liv said. "We saw her come through the portal. The resistance is scouring the city for her."

"No." Philip cast around the room. "She's in here. Down in one of those cells. The priests caught her, too."

Everyone dropped what they were doing and sank to the floor around the seven remaining oubliettes. Fi glanced at the door. This was taking too long. They were going to get caught. They needed to go. Now.

"Here!" Eb whispered. They pried the lid open, lowered the ladder, and two men climbed below. When they returned to the surface, Dr. Hibbert crawled out with them. Her braid had come undone, and she squinted against the daylight.

"Liv, Arvid. You came for me!" But if she thought she might find a sympathetic ear among them, she was wrong. Arvid glared, Philip fumed, and Liv tapped the crowbar against her palm, begging Dr. Hibbert to give her a reason to turn it into a weapon.

"Can't you see I'm a prisoner too? I'm not your enemy. I did what I did to keep the priests out of Earth. To save my whole world. You would have done the same. You know it's true. Arvid? Liv?" Her arms raised in a gesture of surrender. "Philip—I never thought the priests were coming back. I didn't bother with any of the precautions you suggested because I truly believed there was no further threat from Somni. I swear—"

"Don't." Philip tightened his grip on his son.

The fifth horn sounded, echoing through the tunnels leading to the chapel.

"The guard will be changing any second," Liv said. "We don't have time for this. Get rid of her—do whatever is needed to keep her quiet. Bash her head in and throw her back down in that hole. I don't care. But we need to go. *Now*."

"Arvid," Dr. Hibbert pleaded. "I never told the priests about your caverns or your rebels. *Think*. You know I'm telling the truth. They would have buried you if I had."

"You're idiots if you think you can trust a word she says," Liv hissed. "If you don't end her, I will."

"Wait—no!" Dr. Hibbert begged.

Liv hefted her crowbar.

"Katherine's alive." Dr. Hibbert's hands dropped to her sides, and she snarled, like a cornered animal. "Kill me and you'll never see her again."

EMBERS

GRIFFIN WATCHED HIS father charge at Dr. Hibbert and the others rush to hold him back. He could hear the shouts, but it was as if everything were happening at a distance, far away from where he stood.

You don't go swimming on the Oregon coast, not without a wet suit. It had only taken one time for Griffin to learn that lesson. When his father had pulled him out of the surf, it had seemed like a lifetime before he could stop shivering. The worst part, though? The skin under his fingernails and toenails had been on fire, as if tiny embers had burrowed beneath each one.

That same feeling of being so cold you're on fire burned through him now. "Mom?" Griffin whispered. He grimaced through the painful thaw.

Griffin stared up into his father's face, searching for answers.

"You told me she was dead." Philip choked on the words, bitter and acrid.

"We had a funeral," Griffin protested.

"All this time—"

Inch by inch, Dr. Hibbert was gathering her cool demeanor and settling it over herself like a cloak, smoothing her frazzled hair, her stained and rumpled stola.

"You kept pushing her to go back in—you kept saying we needed more, but you knew they were on to her. You gave her up, didn't you? Didn't you?"

Dr. Hibbert dusted off the backs of her hands. "I did."

"What?" Griffin shrieked. His voice echoed in the stunned chapel. He lunged at Dr. Hibbert, but his father's arms closed around him, holding him tight to his chest.

"You think you're so smart," Griffin spat. "You think you know all the answers. You think you can't trust anyone but yourself. But you're wrong. Thinking like that—it only makes things worse." The embers caught and flared into flame, burning from the inside out, burning itself up. Griffin sagged against his dad. "My mom would have helped you. Together, you could have found a better way than your stupid plan. You should have trusted her."

Dr. Hibbert pulled what was left of her braid over her shoulder. "Like it or not, the deal I struck worked. I convinced the priests that they had all they needed between the silica and Katherine's vast knowledge of glass. Apparently, though, they discovered that it wasn't an understanding of theory and history that they needed. If they were going to construct more portals, they needed someone who actually worked glass, whose hands knew how to shape it and could bend it to their will. Don't you see? I saved all of us."

Dr. Hibbert ticked her head to the side. "Except Katherine. She was a necessary sacrifice. But she understood the risks she took."

"She didn't expect to be betrayed by one of us!" Liv shouted back. "Come on, Philip. She's lying. Katherine is dead."

Dr. Hibbert sighed. "When the alarm sounded the other day? The priests never did plan on restarting their invasion of Earth. They couldn't. Katherine's block on the lens is still intact—the priests can't go through the portal to Earth. None of us can, now. Unless, that is, someone here knows how to remove the block?" Dr. Hibbert quirked an eyebrow in Philip's direction.

"It was a trap. All they needed was to lure a skilled craftsman to the portal, where they could draw him through. They were after you, Philip, all along. I didn't know, I swear. I tried to keep your son out of it—and I could have, if only he had listened to me." She threw her hands in the air, and her voice dropped to a savage whisper. "Why do you think I'm here? I don't actually want the priests figuring out how to make new portals."

"Enough!" Philip shouted. "Where is she?"

"Philip!" Liv was practically screaming. "It's a trap. We can't trust her. You know that."

A scuffle sounded in one of the hallways, and then a crash. Shadows flickered across the walls, rapidly approaching the chapel.

Philip lifted his shoulders in a defeated shrug. "I have to know, Liv. If there's even a chance—"

"We need to go," Arvid interrupted. "Scatter!"

But before they could reach the door, a priest and his soldiers swept into the chapel. Magic rolled off him in thick, peppery waves. When no one even flinched, the priest's face grew tight with rage, and the soldiers stepped forward to protect him. Shouts rang out, and the chapel erupted into chaos. The soldiers were outnumbered, but their weapons came into their hands like they belonged there, and soon it was the rebels who were backed against the wall, dodging blows in a fight they were quickly losing.

Fi glanced over her shoulder. The door to the hallway was open just enough for her to slip through. She could sneak away, and no one would miss her. That's the thing about being a kid in a war meant for grown-ups—you're easy to overlook. Fi sidled one step closer to the exit.

The priest circled around them like a cat stalking its prey. In the center of the room, Griffin and Philip huddled together, holding on to each other while the world stormed around them. Griffin shut his eyes tight, bracing for the moment when someone would try to tear him away from his dad again.

Fi paused. She felt a pang beneath her ribs and a wobbly sensation at the back of her knees. This was it for Griffin and his family. They were never going to make it out of here.

The priest continued to circle. He crossed in front of Fi without even glancing her way. He had his back to her as he moved in front of the hole in the floor— the oubliette that had been Philip's prison.

Fi wasn't very big. She'd never been trained to fight. But there was one particular kind of blow she had mastered. She slipped the paddle out from under her sash, gripped it, and, like she'd always wished she could, swung.

The metal shaft hit the back of the priest's knees, and they buckled, pitching his weight forward. His arms pinwheeled, grasping for a handhold as his body tumbled toward the oubliette. His head struck the grate with a *clang* that echoed like a bell in the chapel. The priest crumpled and dropped through the hole.

Fi leaped into the air, whooping in satisfaction. As if a switch had been flicked off, the soldiers blinked, their faces flushed, and they shook themselves out of their magicked haze. They backed away from the fight, blinking in alarm at the unfamiliar sound of their own thoughts in their heads. Footsteps echoed in the hallways, along with the telltale swish of priests' robes.

"We won't survive a second fight," Arvid bellowed. "Run!"

CHAINS

PHILIP CAUGHT DR. Hibbert by the elbow. "Take us to Katherine. Now." And with no choice but to trust her, Griffin, Fi, and the rest followed Dr. Hibbert into the tunnel on the left. They rounded a corner and thundered down a flight of stairs to a low tunnel with torches set into the walls.

None of it was on the map Fi had studied so carefully. She glanced back over her shoulder at the rectangle of light trailing down the stairs. This was not part of the plan. She gripped her paddle in both hands and followed the others. At the bottom of the stairs, the tunnel took a sharp turn, and they ran straight into a locked door.

Griffin tugged at the handle, rattling the door on

its hinges, but it wouldn't budge. "Mom! Are you in there? Mom!"

"Get back," Eb said. He got a running start and rammed the door with his shoulder. The hinges groaned and the resin window cracked, releasing a cloud of heat into the hallway. He backed up again for a second try.

"Wait—" Fi yanked the ring of keys from her sash. Her hands trembled, the keys clanking together, as she fitted one after another into the lock.

"Hurry," Griffin pleaded.

The first key was no good. The second and third turned halfway but wouldn't go any farther. The fourth key slid into the lock and turned in a full revolution. The door clicked open, and heat poured out of the tiny room.

Through the waves of heat Fi saw the silhouette of a woman gripping the worktable behind her. She was terribly thin. The skin under her cheeks sagged, and the bones of her shoulders and hips prodded the worn stola that covered her. Broad metal cuffs clanked around her ankles, leading to a bolt secured to the wall.

"Philip?" Her voice scratched like a rat at the door. "Griffin, is that you?"

Griffin looked into her face. It had only been three

years, but she seemed to have aged a decade for each one. The mother in his memories was full of life— round cheeks and bouncing black hair, with deep laugh lines framing her mouth. This woman looked nothing like Griffin remembered, but it was her, all the same.

She was alive.

He crossed the room, one timid step in front of the other. He wanted to crumple onto the floor. He wanted to collapse against her, but he held back. She looked so fragile.

With a cry, Philip was beside them. He swept his arms around Katherine, holding her up as much as holding her to him. Griffin buried his face in the gap between his mother's ribs and his father's stomach. He couldn't remember a day that wasn't shadowed by grief. And now, for the first time in years, he could breathe without feeling like his chest was going to collapse. They were together. Nothing else mattered.

Fi scanned the room. Just like in the cavern, a brick box filled with fire waited in the corner. A round machine low to the ground shook, a coarse block of glass trembling over a piece of wet, sand-covered paper. Calipers and molds, gloves and Dremels were scattered all along the worktable.

"Fi," Liv whispered. "We have to go. Eb and I are taking Hibbert back upstairs. Come on."

Fi shook her head. "I'm staying with Griffin."

"Fi."

"I'm staying."

Liv grimaced. "Make it quick." And she pushed Dr. Hibbert ahead of them, along the narrow hallway and back upstairs.

Arvid knelt beside Katherine's feet, gingerly lifting the shackles and studying the locks. "The keys, Fi. Hurry!"

Fi tossed the key ring across the room, and Arvid began the slow process of fitting the keys into the lock, one after another. "It isn't working," he muttered. "We don't have the right one."

Griffin pulled himself away from his parents' embrace. Neither he nor his father was leaving this room without his mom. He dashed over to the workbench, sifting through the tools, searching for something to break the locks or snap the chain. He slammed his hands against the workbench and turned toward the fire burning in the glassmakers' kiln. The heat swept over him, licking his face like an old friend. He might not be as cunning as Dr. Hibbert. He might not know how to weigh the scheme of a revolution in his mind like Arvid or Liv, but fire and glass—that he understood.

"Dad!" he shouted. "Come on. The chain is a soft metal. We can burn the links off." Griffin grabbed a glassblower's pipe from the worktable and handed a second to his dad. Together, as they had done so many mornings in their little studio by the sea, they thrust the long steel poles directly into the fire. When the tips of the metal rods were glowing red, they crossed back to Katherine's side.

"Hold still," Philip whispered, pressing the red-hot metal against a single link in the chain. On Katherine's other side, Griffin did the same. Rushing back and forth between the fire and the chains that held her captive, they worked until the links were weakened by the heat.

"Back up, everyone," Philip ordered. He swung the rod over his head and, in a burst of sparks, brought it down on the chains. The metal snapped, and Katherine skittered free. Griffin let the rod drop to the floor with a clang. His breath wobbled out of him, and he fell against his father's side.

"I've got her," Arvid said as he lifted Katherine onto his back.

"Let's go!" Fi snatched the ring of keys from the ground. They thundered up the stairs and through the winding corridors. When they reached the chapel, it was silent. The priests and their soldiers were gone. Fi peered into the corridor. She stepped out into the open. For the first time since she had arrived in Somni, the rectory was completely empty.

27

THE GLASSMAKER'S PUZZLE

THEY RUSHED THROUGH the corridors toward the servants' exit, grabbing anything they could use as a weapon while they ran—knives and hammers, candlesticks and wrenches. The only sounds were their own footfalls and ragged breaths bouncing off the brick walls. There was a scuffle at the side door, and when Fi dashed through a moment later, she had to leap over the bodies of two unconscious soldiers.

When they reached the other side of the wall, they ran straight for the servants' quarters. Liv stood in the center of it all, gathering the resistance to her.

"We're taking Philip back to the caverns with us," Arvid said in between gulps of air. "You take Katherine and Griffin and send them home."

"What?" Griffin shrieked. He tried to yank his

father free of Arvid's grasp. "No! Dad, we have to stay together. Tell them!"

Arvid frowned. "*Think*, Philip. The priests kidnapped Katherine, and then you, for everything you know about glass. Tell me—how long will it take for them to realize your son knows almost as much? How long until they begin hunting him, too? Liv, you have to get Katherine and the boy out of Somni. As long as they're here, they are in danger. All of us are."

"No—Dad!"

Philip knelt in front of Griffin and placed his palms on either side of the boy's cheeks. "I need to finish this—I need to fix the portal so Somni can never attack Earth again. And your mother needs a doctor. Will you stay with her? See that she gets home safely?"

Griffin wanted to bang his fists against his father's chest, kick and scream until he stopped talking crazy. But his mom looked so tired and so frail, the metal cuffs still cutting cruelly into the skin at her ankles. A sigh quivered through him. "You come home, right away. As soon as you're done."

"I promise."

Tears streamed down Griffin's face and closed off his throat. He pulled out the journal and handed it to his dad. "I kept it safe, just like you said."

Philip tucked the journal into the pocket of his ragged flannel shirt. "I'm so proud of you, Griffin." He looked up to where Katherine smiled weakly down on the two of them. His words stopped, and he cleared his throat a few times before he could speak again. "I love you both more than anything in the whole world—more than anything on any world."

Griffin backed away and reached up to take his mother's hand. He didn't care that his nose was running or that he was making awful choking, wheezing sounds while everybody was watching. He only cared that the tears flooding his eyes were making it hard to see his dad raise his hand high in a last wave before he disappeared around the corner.

Liv lifted her fingers to her lips and whistled three short blasts. The sound was echoed in the servants' quarters, and then again in the rectory and from deep within the temple. The daylight was fading, and shadows blended together as, all around, buildings emptied, and the Vinean resistance flooded the streets.

Liv hopped onto the nearest bench and shouted over the crowd. "This is the day we've been waiting for. Don't lose your nerve now, and don't get distracted by revenge. Fight your way to the tower. Whoever gets through the portal first—sound the alarm.

The resistance back home has been waiting for years for our signal to attack the fort." She paused, and a fierce smile crept across her lips. "We're going home."

A cheer erupted from the crowd. Liv thrust her crowbar into the air. "For Vinea!"

"Vinea!" the crowd roared.

The sound echoed off the buildings all around them. It thrummed through Fi's chest, pulsing and swelling until she thought she would burst. It was here. After all those years spent waiting, the time to fight back—the day when she would finally get to save her family—was here.

They hefted their shovels and mop handles, hammers and trowels, and the sprint for the temple began. Fi was swept into the crowd that swarmed across the amphitheater and up the stone steps. She broke into a cold sweat as she ran. Her mouth was dry, her tongue clicking against the roof of her mouth. This was it.

The resistance streamed up the steps and through the broad doors. The priests were waiting for them, row after row of men in blood-red robes. Each one clasped a heartstone ring in his fist, the air filling with the peppery smell of magic. But the Vinean charge didn't falter. The priests' faces shifted from scorn to alarm as they reckoned with the years of cunning that had allowed their servants to rise up against them.

Shouts and the clash of steel on steel rang through the temple. In the wake of the priests' shock, the resistance felled the first line of priests and over-whelmed the soldiers. They ripped the heartstones from the priests' fingers. They stripped off the straps and tubes that held the dreamers in place, lifted the frail bodies down from their alcoves, and settled them into the pews.

Fights waged all around, but a path opened down the center aisle, and Fi ran for the tower rising out of the apse like a beacon. She was so used to going through life unnoticed—it had never occurred to her that one of soldiers locked in battle on either side might train his weapon on her.

She'd barely registered the studded club swinging toward her head when Eb stepped into its path. He thrust his table knife between the soldier's ribs just as the club connected with the back of his head. A sound like a tree splitting down the middle echoed through the nave. The soldier screamed, falling back, and Eb dropped to the ground, motionless. Fi skidded to a stop.

"No!" she shrieked. She crouched down beside him, her hands fluttering, useless to help. His face was impossibly pale, creased with pain. "What did you do that for? *Eb!*"

He struggled to raise his eyelids. "Go," he wheezed.

"I'm not leaving you like this—there's got to be someone who can help. I don't know anything about healing. Why did I never bother to learn—"

"Fionna," Eb gasped. "There is more for you on the other side. If I helped get you there . . ." And then there was a long pause, so long, Fi began to worry he'd already left her. A trickle of blood dripped off his earlobe, staining the stone beneath his broken head. His lips parted ". . . then I have done my part."

"But, Eb—"

His eyelids sagged closed. *"Go."*

Fi's whole body shook. She stumbled to her feet, sobbing, and ran toward the tower. Her arm was wet. She looked down, confused. A long gash traced her forearm, and blood dripped from her elbow onto the bricks below. She didn't even remember being struck.

Griffin had almost caught up with her. Katherine's arm was slung over his shoulder, both of their faces tight with strain. Liv was just behind them, dragging Dr. Hibbert with her.

Fi sprinted up the spiral steps that led to the top

of the tower, then, gasping for breath, leaned over the cast-iron railing. "Griffin!" Her voice was sharp with panic. "I need you!"

But he didn't budge, afraid to leave his mother's side even for a second. Fi paced the landing. She groaned in anguish. Her heart felt like it was splitting apart. Her mind kept replaying the moment when the club crashed into Eb's skull. And that sound—

She stepped to the window, clenching her fists until her fingernails broke the skin. She opened her eyes as wide as she could, willing them to see anything but that terrible moment. Above her, the eight beams swept across the city and over the wastelands beyond. She'd only seen Somni from this height once before, on the day she'd first arrived. Her gaze traveled over the shadowed neighborhoods that curved like insect burrows in and out and in on themselves again. The beams swept past, lighting up the thin clouds and the flat, barren ground beyond.

Fi gasped. She gripped the windowsill and leaned out as far as she could. There, so far out she had to squint to see it, a trail of dust curled into the sky. In the distance, a line of people scoured the ground, guards watching their every step. Hope took Fi by the throat. She grasped the sill so tightly she slipped, her knuckles scraping against the coarse brick. Blood skimmed the surface of her skin, and she backed away from the window.

She leaned over the railing a second time. Griffin and his mom were coming, but painfully slowly. "Hurry!" Fi shouted.

"Come on, Mom. We'll go up together."

"You go first." Katherine gasped for breath. "I'll be right behind you."

"No—I'm not leaving you." Griffin's voice faltered.

"All those people back there, fighting—they're counting on us to open the way to Vinea, and to Earth. We have a job to do."

"But I don't even know what you did to block the portal. I don't know how to fix it."

Katherine brushed a lock of thick brown hair out of Griffin's eyes. "You *do* know. Trust, Griffin. Trust in everything your father and I have taught you. Trust yourself." She gave him a gentle push. "Go."

Griffin ran up the tower steps. On the second-to-last landing, he paused at the window, grabbed the zigzag-shaped block of wood off the windowsill, and moved straight for the huge brass gears.

"What are you doing?" Fi shrieked.

Griffin didn't answer. He stood directly below the gears, watching them turn. There was only one way inside the lens, through a gap in the rotating metal plating. He waited until the gap appeared overhead, and then he thrust the block of wood between the pegs. With a groan, the gears stuck. A triumphant smile broke over Griffin's face, and he pulled himself up inside the lens.

Nobody was allowed up there, except the lighthouse keepers. Griffin had always loved it when his dad had let him crawl inside the lens with him. The outside world went fuzzy at the edges—it was magic. The kind of thing he'd always thought of as magic before, anyway. Everything, all around you, was glass. You had to squint, sometimes, it was so bright, six-hundred-something prisms winking in the sunlight.

Griffin spun in a slow circle, examining each panel. Someone who didn't work with glass every day might think the panels were all the same. You had to know what you were looking for. The block his mom had installed would be something to stop the light's amplification. *Think.* The smallest circle in the bull's-eye, then, where all the refracted light was concentrated into a single beam. He dropped to his hands and knees and ran his fingers along the stepped edge.

"Griffin!" Fi shouted. She pressed her hands

against the glass on the other side. Her voice sounded like she was underwater. He could barely see her— Fi's outline was broken up and hazy, but the tension in her voice cut through the glass between them. "Will you hurry up?"

Griffin ground his teeth together. The circular prism in front of him was smooth and unaltered. He moved to the next, and then the next. He found what he was looking for on the fifth try: a thin glass collar ground to a tapered edge that slid over the round prism. You couldn't see it if you looked from inside the lens or out, and you couldn't feel it unless you knew that lens as well as you knew the bumps and grooves of your own skin.

Griffin slid the collar off and held the thin circle up to the light. The design wasn't in his father's notebook or in any of the drawings. Griffin lowered himself through the opening in the floor, and then he dropped the rest of the way, his feet clanging against the metal landing below. He jumped up and took the small flight of stairs up to the lantern room two at a time.

"Before the rest get up here, come here, quick," Fi whispered.

"What?" Griffin peered over the edge to where Liv was shoving Dr. Hibbert ahead of her and somehow also helping his mother climb higher and higher. "Fi, there's no time. We've got to get these portals open."

Fi closed the distance between them until she was toe-to-toe with Griffin. "I helped you. You owe me. Come *on*."

Griffin swallowed. "Okay, but quick."

"Oh, *now* you're in a rush." Fi handed him a folded rectangle of map paper. She grabbed his shoulders and positioned him beside the bull's-eye leading to Arida. "Do exactly what I do."

She raised the paper in front of the one leading to Glacies, blocking the beam, and then she lowered it again quickly. Up and down, up and down in a rhythmic pattern, so the beam stretching over Somni flashed like an alarm signal.

Griffin matched her movements. "Why are you doing this? Who are you signaling? Does Liv know?"

"I already got Somni, Maris, and Vinea while you were in there." She dragged Griffin past the eighth bull's-eye leading to Stella. It was empty, the rectangular frame missing its glass. Fi stopped in front of the one that read CALIGO.

"These are the last two. Come on, hurry." Once more, they blocked the beams in steady intervals. Whatever message she was trying to send with her blinking lights, it would stretch all the way around the tower and travel straight out to the horizon. Fi dropped the papers behind her just as Katherine, Dr. Hibbert, and Liv climbed up into the lantern room. Griffin reached out and clasped his mother's hand. His eyes were bright, still marveling that she was there with him. "Let's go home."

Katherine squeezed his hand, and she moved in front of the bull's-eye leading to Earth. Far below, the stairs pounded with footsteps. Fi leaned over the edge. Flashes of red and black speared through the holes in the grate.

"They're coming! Quick!"

The soldiers were nearly to the second landing. Fi groaned—they must have come in through a different entrance to the temple. All that time, mapping the city so meticulously—what else had they missed? Liv pulled the crowbar from her sash and moved to block the top of the stairs. To everyone's surprise, Dr. Hibbert took the hammer from Katherine's hands and stood shoulder to shoulder with Liv.

Just then, the bull's-eye behind Griffin began to shift—not the one to Vinea, and not the one to Earth, either. The panel wavered and swirled, the yellow of the reflected Somnite sky mixing with the sea-green glass.

"Are you doing that?" Fi screeched.

Melanie Crowder

"No—it's not me!"

Liv swung her crowbar left and right, landing dull, cracking blows. Dr. Hibbert gripped the hammer with both hands and chopped as if the oncoming soldiers were nothing more than firewood. They had the advantage, the higher ground. But there were too many soldiers, and eventually, Liv and Dr. Hibbert were pushed back into the cramped lantern room.

The whites of the priests' eyes flashed, and the red of their robes swished. Fi darted out of the way of a hand that reached out to grab her by the neck. She took a step toward Griffin, and in that instant the swirling glass reached out. The soldiers closed in and the priests loomed, but they were too late.

Fi lifted her hand in front of her face, staring in disbelief. The edges of her skin wavered, glowing and insubstantial. She felt the pull of the portal like a tractor beam tugging at her organs. If Griffin hadn't opened the portal, then who?

The whole world went silent in a roar of light, and the noise all around her, and the glass in front of her eyes, and the floor below her—everything except Griffin's hand in hers, was gone.

AN ENDING, AND A BEGINNING

FI DIDN'T WAKE so much as she became gradually aware of air passing in and out of her lungs, and of worry, like tiny bolts of lightning flashing across her mind. *Did the raze crews get her signal? Was it enough? Or were they powerless to do anything even if they saw it? And what about Liv? Was she hurt? And—oh no. No—Eb.*

A sharp cold stung her skin. Shivering. She was shivering.

Fi curled her fingers, and there, at last, was something familiar. Griffin's hand gripping hers.

She opened her eyes.

Everything was mist. It pooled under her, lifting her aloft. And it tickled. The mist hovered like a nursemaid over a gash in her arm and the torn skin on her knuckles. It washed over Griffin's cheeks until his eyes blinked open. And it cradled Katherine like a stream welcoming a wilting flower.

Fi sat up.

They were in the tower, but this wasn't Somni. She crawled to the gallery windows, raised up onto her knees, and peered outside. Clumps of structures stretched out over the mist like an archipelago: nest-like homes and open-air markets, vertical gardens and elaborate mews on the horizon. Fi watched as a raptor sped like an arrow, turning his talons up at the last minute to grasp the falconer's arm. Smoke wafted above the ashes of a funeral pyre burning in the distance.

The day was bright—the mist collected the light of newborn stars and dying ones all the same. It cradled the light inside itself until it gleamed. Half the sky was white, made up of layer after layer of mist, and the other half was the hungry black of space.

Behind Fi, Griffin shot up, looking frantically around him. He reached out and brushed the hair away from his mother's brow. Katherine lay in the mist as if she might sleep forever. Griffin shook her arm, and when she didn't wake, he shook even harder.

"Mom, wake up!"

Katherine's eyes fluttered open, and she struggled

to prop herself on her elbows. *Oh*, she mouthed, and when she reached a hand up, both Griffin and Fi hurried to help her stand.

"Oh." This time the word moved past her lips and onto the sodden air. She crossed to the gallery door and opened it wide, stepping onto the narrow balcony and gripping the railing. The mist pooled around her feet, nudging her toward the edge.

But she didn't step up and over. She reached behind her and gathered the children close. *"Look."* Katherine's voice, still raw from disuse, trembled in awe. "We've been called to the mists of Caligo."

Fi groaned.

"What?" Griffin cried. "We were supposed to go home! I promised Dad I'd get you to a doctor."

"It seems that someone had a different idea." Katherine smiled down at her son. She traced the thin line of his jawbone with her thumb, just as she had imagined doing every day for the past three years. "Do you remember the story I told you about this world?"

Griffin nodded. It was so surreal, hearing her speak about the memories he'd clung to like the crumbling edge of a cliff. He leaned over the railing, looking for the ground that should have been there, at the base of the tower. But there was only mist.

"Give me your arm, Fi," Katherine said, and she lifted the girl's hand, turning it over to reveal the soft flesh of her forearm with its ribbons of green veins overlaid with trails of dried blood. A tendril of mist wrapped around the elbow, and Katherine shooed it away. The mist retreated in overlapping swirls, revealing a pink line of raised skin.

"But—" Fi rubbed at the new scar. That had been a nasty gash a few minutes ago. "How?"

"You see?" Katherine said to her son. "The mists are healing. Just being here will do me more good than any hospital on Earth. I'm feeling stronger already."

Griffin relaxed against her side, and he grabbed her hand where it draped over his shoulder. The sharp curve of her ribs against his cheek, the pattern of her breath on his hair—Griffin had spent so long missing those very things that a ribbon of shyness tied his tongue.

Beside them, Fi tensed. "What's *that*?"

Griffin and Katherine looked past her pointing finger to where a shallow boat floated steadily toward them, riding the currents of air. At first it seemed like nothing more than a shadow in a seam between layers of mist. But as the boat left the aerie in the distance and wove closer, the wind nudged the bow, and light glanced along its pea-pod shape. The boat swung broadside as it drew near; now that it had reached its destination, it lay perfectly still, not tempted by the swirling mists anymore.

Griffin tilted his face up to look at his mother. She didn't seem tired anymore, and though she was still far too thin, the chill in the air had brought color to her cheeks. Or maybe it was the thrill of it all.

Griffin laughed. He'd forgotten that look on her face, how even the barest hint of adventure made her whole being light up. Katherine's face was flushed, the tops of her cheeks apple red. Griffin took his mom's hand and laughed again. He couldn't help it. Neither one of them was any good at hiding their emotions. And maybe that wasn't such a bad thing, after all.

When you're floating along a river, you can feel the current beneath you, tapping against the underside of the boat, nudging you away from boulders and drawing you down into churning holes below. This boat trip was marked by the absence of those things. Nothing bumped or pulled at them, nothing knocked against the sides or lapped against the stern. And there were no paddles or oars of any kind.

The boat simply slipped its mooring and turned

about, climbing steadily upward against the airstream. Griffin and his mother leaned over the edge, marveling at the winged creatures that flitted and flapped in the space above and far, far below them.

The aerie was a single platform with a round structure like a swallow's nest at its center. The boat drew near and slowed. A boy knelt on the platform a few paces in front of rows and rows of men, women, and children, their heads bowed in deference. Their skin rippled and shifted in concert with the mists that slid all around. Behind them, a dozen women stood together. Fi squinted, peering more closely. It wasn't just the starlight glimmering off their skin, or the weight of her wishing that made it so: The women glowed, the strength of the green blood in their veins potent enough to light the mists around them.

Fi trembled. Her cheeks were wet, tears streaming down them and soaking into the collar of her stola. "Greenwitches? Here? But . . ." Her words drowned in her own tears.

"Welcome to Caligo," the kneeling boy said with a gesture of welcome to the girl from Vinea and the mother and son from Earth. He wore a cloak of white feathers over a bald head and bony shoulders. His knees and toes were pillowed in mist. "This is my first official act, summoning you three."

Fi swallowed, swiping the backs of her hands across her cheeks. The shock fell away with the last of her tears.

"You're the Levitator?" Griffin frowned. "But you're just a kid."

The boy ducked his head, hiding a grin. He gestured to the funeral pyre far below. "I *was* merely a child, but when the Levitator left us (may he rest in peace forever) his sight and strength fell to me."

"And you're going to help us?" Griffin asked. A new feeling bubbled up in his chest—something he hadn't felt in so long he almost couldn't put a name to it. Something light and airy. *Hope.*

"We were always meant to work together. Somni and Vinea, Earth and Caligo." He nodded in deference to Katherine. "The winds are changing direction and picking up speed."

Griffin scraped his fingernail against the calluses on his palm, where all that work in the glassmaking studio had toughened the skin and strengthened the muscles beneath. On one side of him was Fi, practically glowing, she was so happy to be in the presence of greenwitches. On the other side was his mother. Not just *not dead* but *alive.* Griffin let out a breath, and for the first time in years, he let his worry go.

There was a gap between the boat and the platform.

He clasped his mother's hand, and, matching her smile with one of his own, together they stepped out onto nothing but mist. When they reached the platform and climbed up onto solid ground, the Levitator nodded once in approval, and he offered a cryptic smile.

"Welcome. We've been waiting for you."

 ACKNOWLEDGMENTS

Seeing this book out into the world was the work of a whole host of people—friends and family who bobbled and bounced my infant twins so I could step away to write, colleagues who gifted me with limitless belief and sharp critique, and the stellar team at Atheneum who waited patiently for these fantastical worlds to spin into being.

And so, a thousand thanks to:

Whitney Walker
Reka Simonsen
Justin Chanda
Audrey Gibbons
Jeannie Ng
Julia McCarthy

Brian Luster

Debra Sfetsios-Conover

Kailey Whitman

Ammi-Joan Paquette

Kathleen Wilson

Meg Wiviott

Kristin Derwich

Cammen Lowstuter

Anna Eleanor Jordan

Annie Walker

Ted Walker

Tiffany Crowder

Stacy Stahl

Shanna Freeman

Justine Lacy

Kelly DePalo

Sandra Galván

Miki Aylesworth

Ben Ervin